I0760477

Queens of the Fae book Ten

FAE'S ENVOY

MELISSA A. CRAVEN
M. LYNN

Edited by Caitlin Haines
Cover by Maria Spada

For the Love of Ham

MYRKUR KINGDOM
NORTHERN VATLANDS
FARGELSI KINGDOM
LOCH VILLANDI
SOUTHERN VATLANDS
ELDUR KING
DRAGUR FOREST
VINDUR CITY
LOCH LANGT
ELDUR DE
TEOTA
SAN

NORTH EASTERN WASTELANDS
KINGDOM
HUNTING LODGE
VALE OF STORMS
FIRE PLAINS
ELDFAL
LENYA
GRIMA KINGDOM
THE BURNING SEA
MINES
VONDUR KINGDOM
UR CITY
THE ROCKY SEAS OF LENYA
THE GRIMA SHOALS

Chapter One
GULLIVER

Cold. Freezing cold air seeped into the throne room at the Iskalt palace. Despite the multiple hearths blazing. Despite thick velvet rugs covering the stone floors. Despite the warmth that normally enveloped the people sitting around the circular table.

Because none of them knew why they were here, except Gullie. Darn Tia for bringing him into this mess. All he'd been able to convince her of was that they had to consult the other royals when they arrived and couldn't just act unilaterally to fix the problem. And a big freaking problem it was.

A gathering of all the ruling royals of the now five kingdoms didn't happen often. There were only two circumstances that could make one of them call on their peers in any official capacity.

An imminent death. Or war.

Gulliver didn't want them to think Tia was dying. Magic, he hoped they didn't assume that. New fear imagined, he paced along the rear of the throne room where all the other plebeians stood. Each had been invited into this meeting for one reason or another. None had royal blood. Well, none except his parents.

"Why am I here?" he mumbled to himself. He understood why his father and mother were told to come. King Hector of Myrkur rarely made any decisions without consulting them first. Sure, Gulliver was a friend of Queen Tierney's—he still couldn't get used to that crown on her head—but that didn't make him one of them. Tia wanted him involved in this, but he didn't see what he could do.

He didn't belong among the lawmakers, the magic wielders, those with the power to hold the kingdoms together or break them apart. Never before had there been a time where they were more united. Yet, a chilling foreboding filled the air.

"Will you stand still?" Griff hissed. "You're putting your mother on edge."

Riona scowled at him. "Speak for yourself. If I were Gullie, I'd be pacing too. Why was he summoned with the rest of us, Griff?"

"Exactly." Gulliver pointed at his mother. "I should be safe in my room here at the palace. It's my right as the queen's best friend."

"It's the middle of the afternoon." Griff did not look amused.

"And?" Gulliver didn't care what time it was. He wanted to curl up and sleep. They had arrived only yesterday and Tia had forced him into her rooms almost immediately to tell him of the news from her father. Before that, he'd been in Lenya as an emissary to oversee the delivery of the newest shipment of crystals. Without one of the O'Shea's, it was a long journey back.

Gulliver caught sight of one such O'Shea as Toby slouched in and leaned against the wall nearest the exit, trying not to be seen. Gulliver hadn't seen Toby much since his boyfriend, Prince Logan, died in a terrible accident in the fire plains. In fact, it would be six months ago tomorrow. They'd both been busy.

He skirted along the wall to reach the prince. "Tobes."

"Quiet." Toby looked at his feet.

Gulliver glanced toward the table, where the rulers of Eldur, Fargelsi, Myrkur, and Lenya chatted amongst themselves, tension thick in the air.

"No one is paying attention to the likes of us." He leaned beside him. "Do you know what this is about?"

"No." So, Tia hadn't even confided in Toby? Were Kier and Gulliver the only ones she trusted now?

"Do you know why I'm here?"

"Not everything is about you."

Gulliver's tail smacked Toby in the face. The prince didn't even flinch. "Don't be rude. I just want to know why the summons my parents received demanded my presence as well."

"I don't know. Maybe you ran afoul of my sister and everyone is here to watch her hang you by your tail."

Gulliver twisted to look at his tail. It flicked like it had a mind of its own. "Don't listen to him. Tia would never hurt you." His cat-like eyes narrowed. He opened his mouth to say something to the prince he knew he probably shouldn't but stopped when the ornate double doors, carved with intricate scenes from Iskaltian history, opened, revealing Queen Tierney in all her regal finery.

For a girl who never wanted to be queen, she sure took to the role magnificently in her ice-blue gown trimmed in silver. Her collar sat high on her neck, clasped at her throat with a silver brooch encrusted with fire opals, matching the one nestled in her strawberry blond hair.

Next to her, Keir Dagnan wore a jacket that matched her dress. They looked like a perfect set, but Gulliver saw it for what it was. A performance. This was the first time in her reign Tierney would host the other rulers, some of whom were her aunts and uncles, and she sure knew how to make an entrance.

For a moment, she met Gulliver's gaze and winked.

"Hello." She reached the long table and released Keir's arm. They took two of the many open seats at the table, leaving their thrones vacant on the dais behind them. "Thank you all for coming." Lifting her eyes to those along the far wall, she smiled. "Please, everyone, come sit. I have called you all here for a reason, and it affects more than just those who sit on thrones."

Thrones Tia continued to refuse to sit on. The last time Gulliver was here, she'd said she still thought of it as her father's seat. Brea and Lochlan were suspiciously absent. They had taken the youngest children to the human realm for some traveling, only returning occasionally to deliver news of the other world.

The only members of Tia's family that remained in Iskalt were Toby and their sister Kayleigh.

Gulliver didn't hesitate, walking forward and collapsing into a chair next to the king consort of Fargelsi.

Myles looked at him out of the corner of his eye. "You could at least pretend to be graceful."

A grin spread across Gulliver's face. "And what fun would that be, Oh great and mighty King Consort Myles?"

Myles rolled his eyes, but Gulliver caught the hint of a smile coming to his face.

Griff and Riona took their seats, as did Toby and a few other dignitaries Gulliver couldn't place. Once they were all seated, there were no more empty chairs. Tierney definitely knew how to plan. And she also knew not a single person would decline the invitation.

Gulliver raised his hand.

Finn, King Consort of Eldur, laughed, as did a few others. King Keir sighed and whispered something to Tia.

She shook her head and snapped back. "What is it, Gullie?"

"I don't think I should be here. Your summons must have been a mistake."

She looked straight at him, her eyes glinting with a danger he knew all too well. "A mistake?"

"Um, yes?" He swallowed. There were few people in this life he feared, but his best friend was one of them.

"Care to withdraw that statement?"

"Leave him alone, Tia." Queen Alona to the rescue.

Tia lifted an eyebrow, glaring at her aunt for only a moment before a laugh echoed out of her. "I'm sorry, Gullie. You're just so easy. Of course you need to be here. We have to discuss an imminent danger, one I already spoke to you of. That's why you're here. Plus, I've decided you are to move to Iskalt and become one of my council members." She cocked her head. "Did I forget to tell you? Oops." Her mouth quirked into a half-smile and Gulliver vowed to wring her neck the next time they were alone. Could he be faulted for committing regicide if the queen in question technically wasn't his?

Tia didn't forget anything. She had a mind like no other, and she knew Gulliver would have declined with a big old 'over my dead body'. Unless she asked him to do it in public. Then, he'd have no choice. His jaw tightened. Guess he was becoming a politician. "It would be my honor, your Majesty." He gave a curt bow and hit her with his best 'you're going to get an earful later' glare.

"Wonderful." She turned to the others. "Again, thank you all for coming. I am sorry for the short notice and for the necessity of sending Prince Tobias to fetch you through his portal rather than allowing you to travel by more ... comfortable means."

"I hate portals," Myles grumbled.

"They're so disorienting." Finn shook his head.

"That is not the point." Tia stood, placing both hands on the table. "I'm afraid we face a problem that affects all fae. We're receiving reports of attacks on both fae and humans accused of cooperating with fae in the human realm."

Silence followed her words, but it only lasted a moment before shouted questions volleyed around the room.

"How is this possible?"

"Who is perpetrating the attacks?"

"How many Fae could there even be in the human realm?"

"How do we stop them?"

Griff leaned back. "Did my brother bring you this news?"

Tia lifted one brow. "Yes. The *King* of Iskalt is still watching out for us, as always." She put a special emphasis on the title her father no longer held. Since he basically forced the crown on her, Tia's reverence for her father had gone up a few notches. She'd told Gulliver she understood him better now that she felt the weight of this kingdom on her own shoulders. He wondered if she regretted all those youthful rebellions, but who was he kidding. It was Tia. Probably not.

Tia held up a hand, magic sparking and crackling from her fingertips. Everyone quieted down.

"Wow," she breathed. "Even works on royalty."

"Tia ..." Neeve, Queen of Fargelsi, prodded.

"Right." Tia leaned forward. Her eyes flicked to Gulliver with a look he didn't understand, but then they moved around the table to each royal in turn. "My father believes the attacks are organized, and from what he's told me, I agree with him."

Griff shook his head. He knew more about the human realm than most fae. "But our features appear human there as long as we use glamours. How do they even know where to find the few fae who've managed to reach the human realm?"

"We haven't figured that out yet. My father believes there are more fae and half-fae there than we ever knew. Their non-human features are more subtle than ours, probably because their blood has been mixed with humans over many generations. And we all know the Dark Fae don't even need glamours to appear human. Their defensive magic does the trick. It seems before any of us were born, there have been fae and half-fae living among humans. It's quite a success story, actually. They must have escaped generations of war here, either via Aghadoon or led into the human realm by an O'Shea ancestor. Then, they bred with the humans and created their own communities. I'd love to study it someday and—"

"Tia ..." Neeve shook her head, steering her back on track.

"Fine, no history lesson. What you need to know is there are likely dozens—maybe even a few hundred—fae descendants in the human realm and they're currently being hunted and murdered. It is our duty to help them."

No one spoke for a long moment before Alona, one of the only humans in the group, sighed. "I do not know the human realm as I should. It is where I was born, but I have never lived there. Yet, I have read as much as I can, and it seems to me that wars are as commonplace there as ice storms in Iskalt. Are we sure these are targeted attacks and not just their usual human violence?"

Tia paused, and Gulliver could see it on her face. She wasn't sure of that at all. "I think it's—"

"Don't think, Tia," Neeve said. "For us to act, you have to know."

"But it's ..." She sighed and slid down in her chair. Movement caught Gulliver's eyes. Keir taking Tierney's hand under the table. "One community has already been targeted. What if it happens to another one?"

"And what if it doesn't?" Alona scrubbed a hand over her face. "Tia, you're young, but I believed in your father when he gave you the crown. You are ready, and yet, you still have much to learn. I hope you will let us all teach you because one day, you will make the best queen Iskalt has ever known."

The words were honest, but even Gulliver knew it wasn't the right time for a public teachable moment. Here, in Tia's own throne room, with all other royals in attendance.

"She is already a great queen," Queen Bronagh of Lenya came to her defense. "She has always shown great care for all fae, even those not of her world. Lenya would have died if it wasn't for her. I wouldn't turn my back on other fae experiencing the same fate. But perhaps we should proceed with caution? We need more information before we can act."

A few others nodded. Across the table, King Hector sat perfectly still. Many had wondered if he was the right man to rule Myrkur when Riona named him king. Of all those present, he knew how it felt to suddenly have a crown thrust upon his head. Neeve should understand that too, but she had always been a leader, even before her father abdicated his throne.

Gulliver kicked Myles to get him to stand up for the niece he'd always adored. Myles sat up straighter and kicked Gulliver back. 'You do it', he was saying. Myles was right. As a reluctant part of her council now, it was up to Gulliver to take her side.

"I think we should send a group into the human realm after these as—fools." He cleared his throat, trying not to lose his cool in front of the most important fae in the realm. "We have to do something to help them."

"No." That was Hector. "Sending anyone who isn't familiar with the human realm risks further discovery. We must protect what we have here. Those fae chose to live among humans. They are out of our reach now."

Gulliver would show Hector out of his reach when he jumped across the table and strangled him.

"Are we all agreed, then?" Griff rapped his knuckles on the table. "We wait for more information from Loch?"

Heads bobbed around the table, and Gulliver vibrated with anger, this time directed at his father. How could he abandon those fae? It didn't matter that they chose to live with humans or that they had forsaken their heritage. They were fae, and they were in trouble. It was their responsibility to care for *all* fae. It was their *only* job. Even when the fae in question lived across the veil.

Everyone stood except for Tia. She sat stone-still in her high-backed wooden chair, her face a mask of the perfect queen. Calm. Confident. But Gulliver knew what brewed behind it because it reflected in him.

"Tia." Alona stopped beside her chair. "Since we're all here, I'm hoping to engage in some trade talks before we go home."

Tia nodded. "Sure, Aunt A."

Alona moved along the table and put a hand on Toby's shoulder. He ripped away from her and fled the room. Her shoulders sagged, and Gulliver couldn't hold on to his anger toward her. Not when she still mourned Logan's death. He was her only son.

They filed out of the room, but Gulliver stayed. He hadn't seen Tia in months before last night and just wanted to hold her and tell her to forget about the rest of them. She was already a great queen. When he, Keir, and Tia were the only ones who remained, he walked up beside her and bent down for a hug. Her head rested on his shoulder.

"I can't believe you'd betray me like that." Gullie patted her shoulder.

"What?" She sniffled and lifted her head. Tears dampened her cheeks, and Gulliver hated them all for making her cry.

"Council member, really?"

"Oh, that." She wiped her eyes. "I just really wanted you here after ..."

"After what?"

"I need you to risk your life for me again, Gul. I have no one else."

Chapter Two
GULLIVER

Gulliver followed Tierney from the throne room into the hall. Keir brought up the rear, stern and silent. None of them talked, but Gulliver had so many questions. He couldn't have heard her right.

They wound through the palace to the royal residence and into the grand sitting room where Princess Kayleigh was with Niamh and Nora, Gulliver's six and eight-year-old sisters.

They all lay on their stomachs, the Myrkurian girls' wings fluttering behind them. There was way too much giggling coming from that corner. That usually meant they were plotting pranks on Gulliver. He loved his sisters very much, but they were trouble.

"Sis." Tierney flopped onto a couch. "Can you take the girls outside?"

Kayleigh pushed to her feet. "It's freezing out there. Ice storm, remember?"

"Right." Tierney looked tired as she rubbed her eyes. "Just go bug Myles then."

Her sister grinned. "Now, that is something we can do. Come on girls."

As they walked by, Gulliver ruffled their dark braids. Niamh pulled his tail and ran from the room, cackling.

Keir sat beside Tierney and wrapped an arm around her. She melted against his chest, her entire body sagging. "I don't like this," she said. "Any of this. I'm supposed to rule over a time of peace. My father, my grandfather ... they were meant to end the strife."

"But there is peace." Gulliver approached the hearth and held his hands out, needing the heat for this conversation. He didn't have a good feeling about whatever came next.

"Between the kingdoms, yes. But this danger in the human realm is big. I can feel it. We can't just ignore it and shut our eyes like the others wish to do."

"They aren't ignoring it," Keir said. "They want to wait and see."

"Do I look like a wait-and-see kind of queen to you?" She glared at her husband. "My father did not hand me his kingdom so I could sit back and let our people—however distant—suffer. If they are in the human realm, they must have been brought there by an O'Shea at some point. I have to trust my ancestors."

"All of them?" Gulliver turned to face her, one eyebrow raised.

She sighed. Her mother's aunt almost destroyed three kingdoms and imprisoned another. Not to mention the atrocious things that aunt's grandmother did to the dark fae. "Don't look at me like I'm nuts, Gullie. Not you. People have been doing that my entire life. I heard the whispers at my coronation. *She's too young, too impetuous, headstrong, and quick to anger.* And they're right about all of it. Maybe it should have been Toby born first, but here I am, and there's no changing it now. So, the question is, are you willing to face danger for me once again?"

"I—" The door slammed open, cutting him off. Griff stormed in, and Gulliver turned to block him from Tia in case he wanted to stop whatever ridiculous scheme she'd thought up.

"So, what's the plan?" Griff stopped right in front of him.

"I don't understand." He eyed his father from his auburn hair to the simple cut of his doublet. He was born a prince, raised to be the king of a foreign nation, and then finally became who he was meant to be in the prison realm. Now, he was protector of the rift in Myrkur but also just a fae living a simple life, who occasionally happened to get drawn into a queen's schemes.

"Let him join us, Gullie." Once Griff sat, she leaned forward to study him. "You made everyone agree to wait and watch for what happened in the human realm. You put a lot of lives in danger."

He sighed. "No, that's what they would have decided, regardless. I only sped them along to a conclusion. No one would have changed their minds. Alona, Neeve, Bronagh, and Hector have to do what's right for their people. Their kingdoms have seen a lot of struggles over the years, and possibly creating another wouldn't have been accepted in their cities. They're cautious now. Conscious of how every choice in this matter could lead to another war."

"And you?"

"I've seen more than they have. I know what it's like to be the one no one wants to fight for. We cannot let those fae down. Plus, I trust Lochlan."

Gulliver had never loved his father more than at that moment.

The doors opened again, and Riona froze in the doorway, her eyes landing on Griff. "What are you doing here?"

He stood. "What are you doing here?"

She straightened, her wings stretching out behind her. "I was looking for Tia and Gulliver, knowing they'd have a plan. As someone who fits in nowhere," she looked behind her, "I know how scared those fae must be."

"And you just weren't going to tell me you wanted to plot with Tia?" Griff crossed his arms.

Riona's look could have cut glass. "As if you'd have told me."

"Guys." Gulliver walked toward his mom and pulled her into the room, kicking the door shut. "Stop being idiots just because you're upset you both had the same idea." He knew them too well to think it was anything other than that. No matter how much they loved each other, they were always competing.

Tia looked between them. "So ... you both want in?"

"Depends on what it is." Riona sat on the arm of the settee.

"Well, I sort of want to send your son into the human realm to find out more about the group targeting fae. He'll have to act human, of course, and it's wicked dangerous. If they find out what you are ..." She met Gulliver's gaze as her words sank into him.

She wanted to send him on a mission to save the fae of the human realm. It was ridiculous.

"What makes you think I'm capable—"

She reached for his hand, holding it between both of hers. "Because you're the only one I trust enough to send. And your defensive magic will protect you more than a simple glamour. To everyone there, you will be no different from any other human."

Why did she have to put it like that? "Tia ..." He couldn't get the words out, couldn't voice what he really thought. Sure, his father sent him places all the time, but the human realm? Alone?

She stood, facing him, and put a hand on each shoulder. "You fought in the war for Myrkur," she started. "The battle of Eldur. You survived the Vondurian dungeon and sailing the Vale of Storms. I don't think there's anything you can't do."

"All of those were with you by my side."

"Isn't there anyone else?" Griff asked, putting a hand on Gulliver's back.

She shook her head. "Not anyone who could pass as human. Gulliver knows their customs well enough—the way they speak and dress. I can't send anyone who hasn't spent time there, and that list is very short. Plus, don't underestimate your son, Griff. He's the best of us. He just hasn't realized it."

Griff's hand slid up to the back of Gulliver's neck. "I could never underestimate this fae. I'm just worried."

Riona pulled him away. "Griff, something brought you to Tia tonight. Someone needs to protect those in the human realm. If Gulliver can do it, we have to let it be his choice. We cannot do the right thing only when it is convenient."

Gulliver could barely hear any of them as he pictured the farmhouse in Ohio. He loved it there, loved the peace. But this wouldn't be that. He'd have to assimilate with humans, talk to them. And yet … he remembered spending every day in Vondur scared for his life, taken advantage of by those in power. If he could prevent other fae from ever experiencing that, he would. "What do I have to do?"

Tia smiled, but there were tears in her eyes. She wiped them away, and her ice queen face returned. "We have intel on the leader of a group we think is responsible for most of the crimes against a community of fae living in a place called New Orleans. Many in the human realm think the deaths are just part of organized crime related to the local gang violence. But we aren't so sure. His name is Claude Devereaux, and his power comes from the number of people throughout the city following him. He has what humans call a militia. Do you know what that is?"

Gulliver shook his head.

Tia continued. "It's when humans prepare for a war they think is coming by waving around weapons and spreading dangerous information."

"So, you want me to what … kill him?"

She shared a look with Griff. "No. Your first mission is just to find enough information that I can bring to the other royals so we can force a more active response from them. We can't have any further overabundance of caution like we saw from them today. However you can get the information, do it."

Tia laid out her plan for them to go over and change as they saw fit. The entire time, Gulliver caught his father casting sad glances at him. His mother was right, though. Others risked their lives to do good all the time. He had before. So, why not again?

He could never say no to Tia.

When they finished, Keir escorted Griff and Riona out, but Gulliver and Tia hung back, not ready to leave each other just yet. Tia turned into him, wrapping her arms around his waist and burying her head in his chest. His tail twisted around her.

"I hate that I have to ask this of you. I tried to find another way, anything else that could help those fae, but I kept coming back to you."

He rested his chin on top of her head. "You're the queen now. The decisions you have to make will be hard sometimes. But I trust you more than I trust myself. If you think this needs to be done and I'm the one to do it, I know that's right." He sighed. "But Tia ... what are we going to do about the others who sat around that table and told you to do nothing?"

She leaned back and looked up at him. "We can't tell them. Not until we have something more concrete. Your parents won't discuss it further for the moment, though Uncle Griff is likely going to make a quick trip to see my father tonight. He'll want the information from the source."

"Eh, he'll probably corner your mother first."

She laughed. "True." Her face sobered. "There is one part I didn't tell Uncle Griff because I don't want it getting back to my parents."

"What? You want me to start a war or something?"

She bit her lip and sighed. "Kind of? Just with one person." She stepped out of his arms and turned away from him. "I'm sending Toby with you."

He froze. "Wait, I think I heard you wrong. Who are you sending?"

She whirled on her heel to face him again. "He's broken, Gullie. I have tried for so long to piece him back together, but it's almost like there's nothing left to heal. He isn't there, and I'm scared for my brother."

"And you think sending him to the human realm, where humans are hunting fae, is the answer?"

"He needs a mission, a purpose. He needs to do something, go somewhere that doesn't remind him of everything he's lost. Moping around this palace and pretending to be fine isn't doing him any good."

"This is insane."

"I know." Her voice rose. "But I don't know what else to do. The truth is, I may have been able to find someone else to go to the human realm, but you are the only fae in the five kingdoms I trust with my brother's welfare."

The idea of not going alone definitely held some appeal, but Toby? He'd seen him today at the meeting. The guy didn't meet a single fae's eyes.

"This could get us both killed."

She shook her head. "I don't believe that. No matter how torn apart Toby is, he'd never put your life in jeopardy. You two can protect each other. He needs you, Gul, just like I always have. Since I was a kid, I had you by my side. Toby deserves a little of that magic too."

"I'm not magic, Tia." He didn't even have magic other

than the defensive kind that would protect his identity in the human world.

She gave him her I-get-whatever-I-want smile, knowing she'd already won. "You have no idea how special you are." She reached up on her toes to press a kiss to his cheek. "I know you won't let me down."

Chapter Three

SOPHIE-ANN

"Are we ever going to get our order, miss?" the annoyed customer called to Sophie as she hustled past his table to deliver coffee and fresh beignets to the people that arrived two tables before Mr. Impatient and his nasty friends.

Sophie-Ann Devereaux hated waiting tables on days like this.

"Your order will be out as soon as it's ready." She rushed back to the kitchen, clutching an empty tray over her chest, as if it would protect her from the stares of all her customers. Sophie hated crowds, and the small cafe near Jackson Square in the French Quarter was always crowded. Pulse pounding in her ears, she ducked into the waitress prep station to get her social anxiety under control and catch her breath. Working was getting harder by the day. Some days, it seemed nearly impossible just to put on her uniform.

Her head ached, and she waited a moment to see if it would get worse or if it was just a result of the intense afternoon heat. Each ache, each roll of her stomach, could mean something dire for her.

"Sophie, we're too busy for breaks! Get your butt in here and deliver these orders!" Vicky, the head waitress sent to Earth just to torture Sophie, shouted at her. Rather than helping out, she stood at the counter, slamming her hand down on the buzzer to tell the waitstaff orders were up. Like they didn't already know they were a table or more behind the demand for fresh beignets, chicory coffee, and all the French pastries the tourists could demand.

Sucking in a breath, Sophie gathered up her wits, pasted a smile on her face, and slid five plates of piping hot beignets onto a tray. She grabbed a pitcher of iced coffee and a sampling of all the best sauces to dip their treats in, and rushed back into the fray.

"Sorry about the wait," Sophie murmured as she set the dishes onto the white linen-covered table at the best booth in the house. Or the worst, depending on who you were. The oversized booth sat in the window overlooking Jackson Square and the streets filled with tourists, artists, and street performers. For those who didn't want to miss a thing, the booth was a prime spot. For those like Sophie, it felt like sitting in a fishbowl, where the world could see every flaw on display.

"Watch it!" one of the ladies at the table shrieked. In her rush to get past the window, Sophie had dropped a plate of beignets all over the pristine tablecloth, where the oil from the fryer immediately spotted the linen. She'd probably have to pay for that.

"I'm so sorry!" Sophie snatched up the hot pastries with her bare hands, wincing at the sting. "I'll get you another order right away."

"It's fine." The young woman sighed, rolling her eyes as she brushed the scattered powdered sugar into a neat pile. "Kind of on par with my day of bridal fittings." Tears swam in her eyes, and Sophie started to panic. Standing here with her head pulsing, she wasn't sure she could handle a crying customer. A bride no less. Sophie was one of those people who cried whenever other people cried. It wasn't sympathy so much as a nervous reaction to not knowing how to handle it.

The woman's companion reached out and patted the girl's hand. "It's been just awful." She shook her head, her eyes full of sadness, like someone had died. "The seamstress stabbed her with a needle and got blood on her beautiful white dress."

"And now, I'll probably die of tetanus." The bride scowled. "And don't expect me to pay for those." She pointed at Sophie's hands.

"Right." The beignets were turning to mush in her hands. "Uh ... I'll be right back."

Sophie ran into the kitchen and tossed the mess into the trash. Her shoulders slumped as she furiously wiped the sticky sugar from her hands. Between the tablecloth and the fifteen-dollar plate of cheap fried dough, she'd probably end up working for free today. Not that she needed the paycheck for anything specific.

She still lived at home with her dad, and she was a low maintenance kind of girl with bigger problems than a less than a perfect afternoon of shopping with her non-existent friends.

Sophie went out to grab the tray she'd left perched on one of the waitress stands. She could never keep track of that stupid thing.

"Seriously, girl, where's our order?" The jerk from earlier gave her a murderous look. "We're starving here."

"Sorry! Be right back." She ran past the table to the safety of the kitchen again. The dining room was like a gauntlet she never seemed to get through unscathed.

"This is the worst job ever." She stood at the pastry chef's counter, tapping her foot and waiting for the jerks' order. Her father thought working at the cafe was exactly what she needed to prepare her for following in his footsteps. He'd even gone so far as to fill out the application for her and called in a favor with the owner—a fact Vicky liked to remind her of at least once a shift.

He thought getting her out of the house would somehow magically make her the daughter he wanted.

Still muttering to herself, Sophie slammed the artfully plated tiramisu onto her tray and marched out to the dining room to deliver the desserts and refill their coffee before the silly boys perished right before her eyes.

"Worst waitress ever," one of the boys said loud enough for the whole restaurant to hear.

Sophie's face flushed beet red, and for once, she found her words. "I'm sorry, but as you can see, we're a bit busy."

"We shouldn't have to pay for this." The meanest of the group pinned her with his stare, and Sophie stammered an inarticulate response.

"Seriously, sweetheart, you might want to consider another line of work because you really suck at this job."

And just like that, she lost her words, turning on her heel, she ran for the kitchen, itching to take her apron off and scream her resignation so everyone in Jackson Square could hear it. But she'd almost made it through her shift. She could last another twenty minutes, and then she'd have two blissful days off where she could stay at home, reading under her favorite old tree in the backyard ... and attend her father's meetings.

"Stupid fae freaks have to ruin everything." She slammed an empty coffee carafe into the machine and punched a series of buttons to set it brewing again. She used to spend all her free time with her dad, hunting through the city's oldest bookstores for treasures and talking about their favorite fantasy books. And her mom ... before she died, they used to cook together on the weekends, making a huge batch of the best gumbo she'd ever tasted. They only used the freshest ingredients they could find at the French Market. They even bought their crawfish from a local fisherman who lived down the street. Thanks to the fae and their dark magic, that idyllic life was over.

"What was that, Sophie?" Vicky came up behind her to add the coffee grounds she'd forgotten before she ruined it ... again. "You know this makes better coffee when you do it right."

"Sorry. I'm a little scattered today."

"Busy days will do that. You just have to take it one task at a time and not let it overwhelm you."

"I'll try that." Sophie wondered why she was being so nice and understanding. Two qualities Vicky sorely lacked.

"Your bridal party just left. Go bus the table and change the linens. The dry cleaning will come out of your paycheck."

Now that was more like the Vicky she knew.

"Yes, ma'am." Sophie grabbed a bin and headed back into the dining room. Truth be told, she'd rather be a bus girl than a waitress. She didn't mind bussing tables since she didn't have to talk to people. Dumping the half-eaten plate of beignets into the bin, she focused on the mindless task. She didn't see the person staring at her through the window until it was too late. As she lifted the bin that was almost too heavy for her, she blew a short strand of blue hair from her face to find the handsome man staring at her.

"Gabe," she muttered under her breath. He was too beautiful standing there watching her with a bemused expression on his face. Too bad the ugly showed through whenever he opened his mouth to speak. She turned away, hurrying for the kitchen to dump off the dishes and buy herself a minute before she had to face her father's second in command.

"I'll finish your last table," Vicky said as Sophie set the heavy bin of dishes on the stainless steel counter for the dishwashers to handle. "I'll see if I can salvage our reputation. Those guys are furious with you."

"They didn't like waiting, but I swear, I didn't make them wait long."

"You have to balance your time better or I'll have to put you on the slower shifts where you won't make as much."

"I understand." Sophie was quick to respond, thinking it wouldn't be so bad. She'd probably still make enough to fund her book-buying habit.

"Go clock out."

"Yes, ma'am."

"And don't call me ma'am. I'm only a few years older than you."

More like a decade or two.

"Yes, ma'am ... er, sorry, Vicky." She headed for the back room to clock out before she grabbed her clutch purse from the office and darted out the door to avoid Gabe. She made it halfway down the alley before she ran into him.

"I guess I should have seen that coming." Her shoulders drooped in defeat. "What do you want?"

His eyes said he wanted her, but as far as she was concerned, that was never going to happen. He just wanted her for the connections she could bring.

"Your father's called a meeting." He ushered her onto the sidewalk.

"We just had one." Sophie quickened her steps. If her father sent Gabe after her, she couldn't escape the summons. He was the most trusted of her father's followers.

"Not a regular meeting. This one's an emergency." Gabe's southern drawl was an odd mix of his father's old creole and his mother's Cajun roots. The leadership was a handful of her dad's most trusted soldiers–his very own militia.

Gabe seemed to vibrate with nervous energy as they walked along Chartres Street toward Esplanade Avenue and the French Market.

"What's the meeting about this time? Have the fae attacked?" Her heart thudded in her chest at the thought. "Is anyone hurt?"

"No. You'll see when we get there." They walked in

silence along the busy streets, the hot summer sun beating down on their shoulders, sweat making Sophie's clothes stick to her skin. It was always hot in the Quarter during summer, but today was sweltering.

"Keep up," Gabe called over his shoulder as she fell behind, unable to match his long stride. Sophie was a petite girl—all of five feet and an inch or two to spare, depending on which shoes she wore. She had to take nearly three steps for each of his, and her heart was flying in her chest by the time they reached the corner of Decatur and Esplanade.

The market was packed today, and the sidewalks swelled with too many people. A panic attack rose up within her as they crossed the street.

Finally, they stepped through the wide gates of her little slice of heaven in the middle of the Quarter. The old Spanish chapel had been converted to a residential home ages before she was born, but when her father moved them here many years ago, it became her oasis. Huge cypress trees shaded the small chapel, and Spanish moss hung from the branches. A high brick wall skirted the property, and as they closed the wrought-iron gates behind them, the noise of the streets faded and Sophie took a deep breath, slowly letting it out.

She left the budding panic attack behind her on the sidewalk. It would be there for her when she left for her shift on Saturday. The courtyard garden blossomed with fragrant flowers and spicy herbs, and the sun shone through the stained glass windows that illuminated the interior of the house in a riot of warm colors.

"Where's Dad?" She frowned at Gabe. Her father spent

most of his time working in the garden or sitting in his favorite patio chair, working on his laptop.

"The warehouse." Gabe nodded to his car. "I'm to take you there in an hour." Sophie turned wide eyes on Gabe, who nodded. "We finally got one, Soph."

Chapter Four
GULLIVER

"Are you sure about this, Tia?" Gulliver shoved an old pair of human jeans into the backpack Griffin had bought him on his first trip to the human realm when he was just a kid. Somehow, he'd been braver then than he was now. Back then, a trip to the human realm seemed like a great adventure. Now that he was the adult in charge of this mission, it seemed like a really bad idea.

"You've been to the human realm so many times, Gullie. You're the best man for the job." Tia took the jeans out of the bag and folded them properly. "Why are you so anxious?"

"Every other time I've visited the human realm I had adult supervision or we just stayed at the farmhouse. I know how to order takeout and get around okay in small towns. I know how to use their weird plastic money, but that's about it. I'm not even allowed to use the microwave because I've blown up three of your mom's applences."

"Appliances."

"See, I don't even know the right names for their magic boxes."

"Electric."

"Tia," Gullie growled.

"Has it occurred to you that I *am* sending an adult? This time, you're the adult, Gullie."

"And that doesn't terrify you?" His eyes grew wide with alarm. "Because it's got me off my food and that never happens."

"You're going to be great." Tia sat down on the edge of his bed, her pale blue dress fanning out around her. "I wouldn't send you if I didn't think you could do it. This is too important. I have a bad feeling about this, Gul. I think there are more fae in the human realm than any of us ever realized, and someone is targeting them. I need you to find out what's happening. That's literally what you do, Gulliver O'Shea. You always know more about what's going on in Myrkur than Uncle Griff or even King Hector. And it's because you're good with people."

"I'm good with Myrkurians." Gulliver gathered up his stone carving kit and a few small pieces of marble with veins of blue cobalt and stuffed them into his pack. He'd make something for his sisters while he was away. No doubt they'd expect something human upon his return. "Myrkurians love me because I am dark fae. Outside of Myrkur, things are a bit difficult for my kind."

Tia laid a sympathetic hand on his arm. "And I hate that. One day it will be a better world where all fae are accepted as equals. But remember, you're going somewhere where everyone around you will see you as a regular person. To them, you'll be human."

"True." Gulliver sank to the bed beside her. "I just hope I don't let you down."

She leaned into him and rested her head on his shoulder. "Well, that would be impossible. You could never let me down."

They sat there for a minute in silence.

"Gullie?"

"Yeah?"

"Why does your duffle bag smell like ham?"

"In case we can't find food where we're going, I, uh ... brought some provisions. The humans' plastic money always seems iffy to me. I always feel like it can't possibly work."

"Mom uses the money cards all the time. It'll be fine." Tierney reached for his duffle bag.

"Wait, don't do that!" But it was too late. Tia had already unzipped it, and she just looked at him like he'd lost his mind. "Do you even know how long it took me to get that bag zipped?"

"Do you really need a ham, a string of sausages, what looks to be two pies, and three loaves of bread?"

"And a pudding." Gulliver's tail whipped irritably behind him.

"Gullie. They have all your favorite foods in the human realm."

"I don't know about where we're going. I found a book on New Orleans in the library, and they have strange food there."

"I'm sure you're going to like it just fine, and based on my own travels in the human world, you can get pizza and hamburgers practically anywhere, anytime."

Gulliver felt a bit better knowing that. "I just ... If I run into trouble, there's no one to ask, Tia."

"Of course there will be. Did you think I wouldn't ask Dad and Uncle Griff to check up on you now and then? Mom and Dad are visiting Montana right now. Mom said they were glamping. I don't know what that means, but it's a marvelous human word, isn't it? They want to keep the kids away from what's going on over there. So I think they're pretty far away from where you'll be, but you should expect a visit from at least one of them after you get settled. They'll let me know if you need anything."

Gulliver let out a sigh. "Okay, but you have to help me zip this back up. I'm still taking it with me."

"I wouldn't expect otherwise." Tia slipped down onto the floor beside the bulging bag, and together they fought with it until it closed. "Did you bring any more clothes with you? I saw exactly one pair of jeans that probably don't fit you anymore."

"There's a shirt in the bottom of my pack. They fit. Sort of. I'm going to need some new stuff once I get there. I'll go to that big scary marketplace in Grafton. You think Myles' mom would take me?"

"Walmart?" Tia shuddered. "I've never seen a marketplace like that anywhere else. It's terrifying, Gullie; don't go there alone. Just call Mrs. Merrick from the farmhouse, and she'll help you with anything you need. You might find some of Toby's human clothes that would fit you now."

"Speaking of Toby, I haven't seen him since the meeting."

"He's probably in his room. We should go check on him. It's almost moonrise." Tierney stood up and tried to lift

Gulliver's food bag onto her shoulder, but it wouldn't budge. "Want me to put a weightless spell on this before you go?"

"Better not. If humans are attacking fae, the last thing I need is something magic I can't explain."

"Good point." She kicked the bag. "You lift it, then."

"Tia, watch my pies; you'll crush them!"

"Let's go find Tobes."

He was in his room, but he hadn't packed. It looked as though he hadn't gotten out of bed yet, and the day was almost gone.

"Toby." Tia sent balls of light into all the lamps in the room. "What are you doing? You're supposed to leave in less than an hour." She flung back the curtains, letting in the moonlight.

"Go away." Toby groaned from somewhere under the furs on his bed.

"No." Tierney tugged the furs aside, leaving him to shiver in the chill of the room. "And don't complain to me that you're cold. You're the one who let the fire die out."

"Dóiteán," she murmured under her breath, and flames leaped to life in the fireplace. "Now, get up. That's an order from your queen."

"I don't care. I'm not going." Toby sat up and reached for the wineskin that sat by his bed, cursing when he found it empty.

"Are you drunk, Tobias O'Shea?"

"Very." Toby got up and went in search of a chamber pot.

"You stink." Tia covered her nose, turning her back on the screen in the corner.

"Go away." Toby stumbled across the room to collapse on the big leather chair in front of the fireplace.

"You're leaving for the human realm. Right now." She lifted her hands, murmuring a few Gelsi spells under her breath, and clothes and supplies started packing themselves into a bag she'd magicked from under the bed. "Don't make me chase you down the hall with my magic, because you know I'll do it." She stood with her hands on her hips, panting with the effort of packing and yelling at the same time.

"Fine." Toby grabbed a tunic from the corner of his room, gave it a sniff, and shoved it over his head. "At least I won't have to listen to you shrieking at me to do something with my life." He snatched his pack and stalked from the room. "Gullie, we're going now. Keep up."

Gulliver and Tia darted down the hall after him. "And just where were you when I spent half the morning packing my belongings? The best friend who is willingly—if not silently—doing as you asked?"

"While you were pilfering food, I was running a kingdom."

"Right." They came to a stop in the moonlit courtyard just outside Tia's study. She still called it her father's study, even after so many months of being queen. Gulliver wasn't sure she'd ever get used to it.

"Oh no, he's already opening the portal, Gullie. Hurry!"

"Wait a minute, Toby. At least let me say goodbye."

But the air around Toby shimmered for a moment before an opening split the atmosphere. "If we're going, let's go already." He swayed on unsteady feet.

"I'm not getting into that thing." Gulliver shook his head. "He is not sober enough to be taking people through portals." He backed up against the stone walls that surrounded the courtyard, his arms over his chest and a stubborn glint in his eye. "Not doing it, Tia. Don't even give me that look. You know what happened last time I went through a wonky portal."

"But that was *my* wonky portal." She pushed him toward the blue glowing light beside her brother. "Toby is better than me. It's not like he'll send you to a foreign world we don't know anything about."

"It's not, is it?" He resisted her pushing, but she was freakishly strong for a pampered queen, and she had him facing the portal far too easily.

"You two mean everything to me," Tia said. "I'm grateful for your help. Just be careful please. And ..." But Toby didn't stick around to let her finish. Without a backward glance, he stepped into the portal, disappearing in an instant.

"Go, Gullie!" Tia shoved him. "Before he leaves you behind."

"Wait, Tia."

"There's no time." With a final shove, she pushed him into the portal. "I'm sorry!" she called after him. "I love you. Take care of Tobes!"

Gulliver didn't get a chance to reply. The portal took him and whirled him around upside down, bouncing him from side to side before it spit him out.

Thudding onto the ground in a spray of dust and gravel, Gulliver groaned, covering his face with his arms, too afraid to look at his surroundings. "Please don't be the middle of a battle. Please don't be the middle of a battle." He peeked through his arms, and the familiar sight of the farmhouse came into view.

"Oh, good." He sighed, lying down flat in the driveway. "It's just Ohio."

Gathering his wits about him, Gulliver stood up, looking around for Toby. He found him under the old oak tree where Tia's sisters had begged their dad for a tire swing. It looked like a death trap to him.

"Toby?" he called out softly, but the prince didn't move. "You okay, Tobes?" He toed him with the tip of his boot. "Please don't be dead."

The prince let out a snore, and Gulliver was both relieved and irritated. "I should leave you here to sleep it off, but I'm scared of the human house. It's too easy to break things." Grunting, Gulliver managed to get Toby to his feet long enough to drape him over his shoulder and get him into the house. They made it as far as the living room, and then Gulliver went back out for their bags.

While Toby slept on the couch, Gulliver searched the rooms upstairs for human clothes that might fit him and lucked out with a few of Toby's things and some of the former king's t-shirts. They were a bit large on him, but Toby's were too small, and he wasn't sure he should try wearing any of Brea's clothes. Humans were funny about things like that.

Finally, he made a plate of ham and a slice of pie from his stash and went to call Mrs. Merrick. Gulliver hated using human phones. He never remembered how to work them. Most of the time it was just easier to go visit the Merrick farm than take the time to work the phone. But Gulliver didn't want to leave Toby alone.

He finally found the number and hit send.

"Hello?" a lady answered the phone.

"Um, hello." Gulliver held the contraption up to his face. "Mrs. Merrick?"

"Yes, dear. Is this a friend of my son's?"

"Er, yes. How did you know that?"

"Caller ID. It tells me someone is calling from the O'Shea farm."

"Oh. Okay, yes, this is Gulliver. I've visited before."

"The boy with the tail, right? Though, you've never shown it in front of me."

"Yes, ma'am, that's me. It's not visible to humans here. Um ..."

"Do you need some help?"

"Yes, please. I have to go to a place ... um, hold on a second. I have the name here." He searched through his pack and fished out a notebook Tierney had given him. "It's called New Orleans. Is that nearby?"

"No, it's quite some distance from Ohio."

"Thank you so much!" Gulliver shouted into the phone.

"No need to shout. Cell phones have excellent connections."

"Sorry!"

"New Orleans is in a state called Louisiana. It's about a thousand miles from here."

"Is that as far as Ireland? I went there once and didn't care for it." Gulliver didn't want to fly in one of the humans' metal birds. It was one of the worst experiences of his life.

"No, much closer. "Have you ever flown before?"

"Yes, though, I'd rather not. My mother and sisters have wings, but I was born with two feet, and I'd rather keep them on the ground if possible."

Myles' mom chuckled and said, "Well, the next best thing is a bus."

"What's that?"

"It's like a big car that carries a bunch of people to the same place."

"That sounds like a good plan."

"All right, I can order you a bus ticket and drive you to the station if that helps."

"I have plastic money."

"Is it one of Brea's cards?"

"Um, yes, Tia gave it to me."

"Perfect. I have the numbers right here on my fridge. I'll use that to buy your ticket. When do you need to leave?"

"As soon as possible."

"Okay, I'm looking at the bus schedule now. There's a bus that will take you nearly all the way there leaving at six a.m. tomorrow. Does that work for you?"

"Yes, ma'am, thank you ... Oh, when is six?"

"It's very early. I can call you to let you know when I'm on my way. We'll have to leave by five to make it to the station on time."

"That would be wonderful if it's not too much of a bother." He didn't want to take advantage of her time.

"Not at all. You can tell me all the news you have about my son's family on the way."

"I can do that."

"Is anyone with you, Gulliver?" She sounded worried about letting him loose in the human world without a guide. A reasonable worry considering it freaked him out too.

"Oh, Toby is with me. I guess he'll need a ticket as well."

"Poor darling. It's a shame what happened to his Logan."

"He's not doing so well. That's why Tia sent him with me—to get him out of the palace for a while."

"That will be good for him. The best thing for a broken heart is activity. Do you need help with anything else? You have human clothes? We can take a quick trip to Walmart if you need to."

"No!" Gulliver panicked at the thought. "Thank you, but no, we have clothes."

"All right, try to get some rest tonight, and I'll see you bright and early in the morning."

"Thank you, Mrs. Merrick." Gulliver ended the call, feeling slightly better about his situation. Once they arrived in New Orleans, that might prove to be a different matter.

Chapter Five
SOPHIE-ANN

Sophie-Ann had conflicting feelings about her father's plans and the organization he'd started to help set them in motion. Yet, here she was in a drafty old warehouse near Lake Pontchartrain. Officially, the building was used by an industrial laundry service, and the whir of constantly running machines filled the air with a familiar vibration.

Unofficially, it was also the headquarters for HAFS, the Human Alliance For Survival. As if they were in any real danger of extinction because a handful of stinking fae decided to make a home in the human world.

She didn't like the fae. They didn't belong here with their unnatural abilities, but even so, most HAFS meetings left Sophie feeling a bit sorry for them.

Her father made her stand at his left while his followers filed in. She'd thought only the leadership group would be here tonight, but more and more people entered. They came from all walks of life. Old, young, all ethnicities, and political affiliations. White supremacists standing side by side with those who'd spent their entire lives fighting for equality.

For humans. That was the point of HAFS. This world belonged to humans. Some of these people should hate each other, but her father brought them together. She should be proud, and she was ... mostly. Before her mother died, he was just another guy working too hard to afford a living in the increasingly expensive city.

Now, he was an icon.

And at the same time, she wasn't sure she recognized him anymore.

The chatter grew as more people entered the room to see what their leaders had called them in for. A captured fae. One of the bad guys.

Only, the man just looked like a frightened human to Sophie. He was on his knees, his shoulders shaking in the dirty and torn shirt he wore. There was a rope around his neck, and Sophie flinched when he moved and it shifted, revealing the red burns on his pale skin.

Sweat-soaked hair clung to his forehead as he lifted his eyes, finding Sophie. "Please. I don't know why I'm here."

The rope jerked, and he tumbled onto his stomach with a groan. Gabe stepped forward, holding the other end. He leaned down. "You don't get to speak to her."

The man's entire body trembled as he sobbed. "Why are you doing this? I haven't done anything."

Gabe kicked him, sending him onto his back. "Fae don't speak here."

"Gabe." Sophie's father put out a hand, calling for calmness. "He's right. He has not been tried for a crime. Yet. We are a just group. Don't touch him again."

Relief bloomed in Sophie's chest, but it didn't last because she'd been around long enough to know exactly what her father's words meant.

The crowd quieted, waiting, anticipating. They came for a show, to witness their work done. There were dangerous people here, but Sophie was protected, untouchable. Alone.

"Welcome, friends," her father said, lifting his hands with a smile. He should have been a preacher with the way he could influence people with his words, his voice. But then, he'd have to believe in something good, and she wasn't sure what he believed in anymore.

"We are here today to do our grave duty." He bowed his head, and the others followed suit. "Let us bring justice to the human race this day. We fight for our wives, our husbands, and our children. We fight for those who do not even know the battle facing them. You see, friends, we are blessed. Our eyes have been opened to the existence of these otherworldly beings. They don't belong here, among us, deceiving us. Our trials will be rewarded."

Each meeting began with a similar opening—one to remind the people that every action they took, no matter the guilt they felt, was entirely right. They were justified in their indignation.

There was a word for groups like this, but it had taken Sophie too long to see it for what it was.

A cult.

Her father was a cult leader, and her mother would be so ashamed.

A smile spread across her father's face. "Now, shall we begin?"

A light above the scared prisoner flickered on, shining directly down on his beaten form. Those nearest to them closed in, making the circle smaller, and others pushed from behind to see the captive, to witness his pain.

Sophie couldn't stop casting glances his way. He looked maybe a decade older than her twenty-one years. Someone who was probably loved, whether he was fae or not. As much as Sophie hated the creatures, as much as she wanted them gone, she couldn't help wondering what this all meant. Fae looked no different from anyone else she'd met. From what they knew, the fae kept families, had culture. These weren't wild animals.

"Who accuses this man of a heritage not of this world?" Her father's question rang in the empty rafters of the room, sweeping over the curious crowd. "Come forward."

A moment of stillness passed before commotion sounded at the back of the group, and a woman pushed her way through. She had blond hair pulled severely back from her scowling face and a very pregnant belly.

"I am the accuser." Her voice was rough, a smoker's voice. As she drew near, tobacco wafted off her.

Sophie's father approached the woman and took both of her hands, speaking gently. "Your care for the human race is a precious thing. We thank you for your bravery. Please take your time and tell us your truth."

Murmured thank yous came from the others. Sophie kept her lips clamped shut.

A tear streamed down the woman's face. "My name is Annette Colewell." She sniffed. "My ... my husband, Henry,

I thought our marriage was based on trust. But the entire time, he was pretending to be something he was not."

"How long were you married?" Sophie's father asked.

"Six years."

"Annette," Henry croaked. "Don't do this."

Annette turned her back on him. "He—I didn't know. I thought I loved him, but I never would have—" She devolved into sobs.

Sophie's father put an arm around her shoulders. "We know. You are a brave and loyal woman."

She wiped her eyes and nodded. "I am. The fae have no place in our world."

"When did you suspect your husband?"

She bit her lip. "Well, he started to sneak out of the house a lot. Sometimes, he claimed to be at work, but I'd call and he wasn't in the office."

Sounded like an affair to Sophie.

Annette went on. "I've known about fae my whole life. My father used to tell me stories, but when I was old enough, he told me the truth. He'd befriended one such creature in his younger years. He didn't know what he was doing."

"He is forgiven for his ignorance," Sophie's father whispered, though the point of that was lost on her since he wore a microphone that broadcast the whisper.

"Thank you," she said. "When I grew suspicious, I followed Henry."

"And what did you find?"

"He had bewitched my sister." Her hand tapped nervously on the top of her belly, probably itching for a cigarette.

"How so?" The calming tone of Sophie's father could

draw the deepest secrets out of anyone. It was why he was so good at this. He knew which buttons to press, how to make people trust him.

Another tear raced down the woman's cheek. "They were in bed together. His magic led her to betray me."

"Annette." Henry tried to crawl toward her, but Gabe jerked the rope, and he fell back. "Honey, what have you done? What magic? It isn't real. There's no such thing as that kind of power. Please believe me. Celeste and I were a mistake."

Sophie wanted to tell her father to stop this farce, that this man wasn't one they were hunting, but she knew how it went from here. One accusation was all it took, one person with a story.

"Dad," she whispered. "I don't think he's fae."

Her father sent her a scathing look and covered the mic on his shirt with his hand. "That is not for you to say. A wife knows her husband, and we can't take any chances."

It was then she realized how much her father had truly changed. He'd rather kill humans than spare fae. All she could do was nod and take a step back.

"This man is guilty, Soph." Gabe's fingers grazed her arm, and she froze, not wanting to make a scene in front of all these people. He was respected in HAFS, a man on high, with only her father more highly thought of. "Accept it."

Her jaw clenched, but she didn't respond. To her, Gabe was nothing more than a young tyrant, one who wouldn't leave her alone.

Her father paced in front of the crowd, arms clasped behind his back and head bowed as if in thought or prayer.

But if it was the latter, something told her God wanted no part in what happened inside these walls.

Annette bent down, saying something to Henry none of them could hear. Then, she disappeared into the restless crowd.

They waited for her father to stop, to speak to them again and tell them what to do. He took his time as Henry yelled, "I'm sorry. I'm sorry. I'm sorry. I won't ever do it again."

Seeing a grown man cry wasn't something a person forgot. The fear, the pain. Also, the hope. He still believed there was a way out of this, that he might be released, battered but alive.

Sophie pitied him.

Her father stopped moving, his face sure. He'd made his decision and uttered a single word. "Guilty."

The crowd of followers roared their approval, and Henry jerked his eyes from Sophie to her father to those cheering on his verdict. He still didn't understand.

Closing her eyes for a brief moment, Sophie tried to breathe, to calm her racing heart. When she opened them again, she was the perfect image of her father's daughter. Cold, ambitious. Also, frail. These people didn't know her. She didn't let them. So, they couldn't see the doubt clouding her mind.

Couldn't see that she held in tears as her father approached his captive, or that her body was only ramrod straight because she couldn't move, despite the wave of dizziness sweeping over her.

Her father looked down at Henry. "Henry Colewell, you have been found guilty of fae heritage."

"You're all out of your minds," Henry yelled. "Fae ...

they're just fantasy." He tried to scramble back, but the rope pulled tighter around his neck, cutting off his air. He gasped for breath, his face turning red.

"I was speaking," Sophie's father growled. "Now, as I was saying. Henry Colewell, you do not belong in this world with your fae blood. God put humans on Earth, and you are an abomination. Your magic is a danger to our survival. On behalf of the Human Alliance For Survival, I sentence you to death."

Henry gripped the rope, trying to loosen it with every bit of energy he had left. Gabe let it go just enough for him to breathe. There was a protocol here.

Her father held out a hand, and Gabe placed a Glock in his palm. He only waited a beat before pulling back the slide and firing a single shot.

Henry Colewell jerked, his head slamming into the concrete floor as blood pooled beneath it.

Sophie hadn't been prepared; she wasn't ready to see the coldness with which her father executed a man on the word of his scorned wife. She stared down into his face, still with shock. His wide-open eyes held no life. Gabe bent to remove the rope.

"Can't lose a good rope." He shrugged with a smile before walking away.

Angry red burns marked where it had tightened around his neck.

Lifting her eyes, Sophie caught sight of Annette leaving through a rear door.

Her father lifted his hands to quell the crowd. "Friends, today we have protected everyone we hold dear. Remember that." What he really meant was that any of those present could find themselves accused if they told others outside HAFS of what happened here tonight. "Go home to your families knowing there is one less creature out there waiting to destroy us."

As the crowd dissipated, her father turned to one of his men. "Have that cleaned up." He didn't point or gesture, but everyone knew what he meant.

When he faced Sophie, all tension faded from his face. "I'm starving. How about you, kiddo? Or do you need to rest? I know this was a lot of activity for you."

She stared at him, trying to see the father she knew. The one who held her when her mother died, the man who cried when Sophie got her diagnosis. What would happen to him once she was gone?

Because that wouldn't be long now. Sophie was sick, and she'd never recover. A part of her still wanted to see if she could save her father before she died.

Chapter Six
GULLIVER

Five in the morning came long before Gulliver was ready for it, but here they were. It had taken too long waking Toby up, too long making him get dressed and eat the delicious thing called a Pop-Tart that Brea stocked. And longer still to get him to glamour himself so the humans couldn't see his fae features. They couldn't just rely on a hat or hood this time.

And now, they were late to the bus station.

"The bus leaves in five minutes and we still haven't found it yet." He tugged on Toby's arm, trying to get him to speed up from the sluggish pace he'd had all morning.

"If we miss this one, there'll be another." Toby shrugged.

"We aren't missing this one." Not for the first time, he wished Tia hadn't saddled him both with figuring out who was killing fae and dealing with Toby. Grief was tricky. It had been months, but there was no timetable for moving on, for returning to a life the person one lost wasn't able to live.

But Gulliver couldn't let it derail the mission Tia defied the other sovereigns for. The mission his father thought he could handle. He pictured his parents' faces, how they'd had so much trust in him. It was time to have trust in himself.

Only getting there might be harder than he'd thought. Gullie stopped when he saw a line of identical busses taking on passengers. "Which one is the bus that goes to New Orleans?" Gullie asked a station employee at the gate.

"First one." She pointed to the shiny silver bus. "Better hurry."

"Thanks." He handed over both tickets and took off running for the bus that was about to leave, yanking Toby behind him.

"Ow, let me go."

"Not until we're on that bus." They waded through the crowd and finally made it to the funny sliding door and the steps leading into the huge human car. "Come on." There were only a few open rows in the back, so Gulliver led Toby toward them, shoving both of their bags under the seats and dropping into one.

"Squishy." He wiggled his butt, trying to decide if he liked the seat or not. He better. It would be his for a while. He'd never seen so many humans so close together, and it sent a thrill through him.

An older couple was sitting across from them, staring. Gulliver averted his eyes to the woman a few rows in front of them. She held a baby in her arms.

"Have you ever seen a human baby?" he whispered to Toby.

Toby only acknowledged the words with a shrug, but Gulliver couldn't help wanting to get closer, to see if that baby was just like his sisters had been—without the wings, of course.

The woman turned in her seat and smiled at him. "Hello." She had thick, dark hair pulled into tight braids, not unlike his mother's.

"Toby." He elbowed him. "A human is talking to me."

"Good for you." Toby pulled the hood of his shirt up over his head. "I'm going to sleep. Don't bother me."

Gulliver returned the woman's smile. "Your baby is cute."

She laughed. "It's a good thing because this creature is a little terror."

"Creature?" He crawled over Toby to reach the aisle and slid into the seat behind her, peeking over the back. "What kind of creature? Does he have wings?" He straightened as he felt his tail twitch. "A tail?"

Her laughter confused him. "You're funny." Her eyelashes brushed down across her cheeks. "Why are you headed to New Orleans?"

"Oh." He rubbed the back of his neck. Tia had prepared him for nosey human questions. "Work."

She smiled. "And taking the bus? How odd."

He shrugged. "Oh, I take the bus all the time. I quite like the ... smell." Smell? Really, Gulliver?

Her nose wrinkled. "You mean body odor and trapped farts?"

"Of course." He hadn't meant to say that. Now, she thought he was an odd man who enjoyed smelling farts. Why didn't Tia tell him that was what humans smelled like after a while? He didn't smell it yet, but something told him he would.

She clutched her baby closer, probably trying to keep it from the stranger behind her. "You're cute."

His face heated. "Um, I, um. What?"

"Gullie," Toby called. "I need you."

Understanding dawned in her eyes, but Gulliver wasn't sure why. He smiled in farewell before rejoining Toby.

"What?" He slumped in his seat.

"Nothing." Toby didn't open his eyes. "It's just ... that girl was flirting with you, and you were acting like a fool."

"Huh?" Flirting? No way. With his feline eyes and tail, Gulliver wasn't quite marriage material to most fae outside Myrkur, where he spent most of his time. He was different and had always been okay with that. Okay with the stares and the whispers. It had gotten better over the years as Iskaltians, Eldurians, and Fargelsians grew used to the Dark Fae, but it was never normal.

Toby shook his head. "You're hopeless. The humans can't see your Dark Fae side, remember? To them, you look just like any other bland chap. Don't worry, though, now she thinks you're dating me."

The bus lurched forward, and he gripped the seat in front of them. "You? I would never in my life ... That would be like dating my sister. Gross."

"I'm not a girl, Gullie."

"No, but you're Tia's twin." Revulsion curled in his gut. The twins were family. He didn't want the humans thinking anything else.

"Why do you care what some random human thinks?" Toby sighed.

"I don't ... I don't know."

"I do. It's because you always need to be liked. Well,

Gullie, you're not Tia's goofy sidekick anymore. Now, you're the main character of this humantale. Sometimes, you're going to have to be as unlovable as the rest of us."

The smell hit Gulliver then. It hadn't taken long for him to realize that the woman described it perfectly. Humans smelled, but when trapped in a metal box together, it amplified their stench.

Gulliver choked on it, trying to picture the open fields of Fargelsi that smelled of Gelsi berries or the clean frozen air of Iskalt. *Breathe in. Breathe out. Don't use your nose.*

Tonight they'd reach their destination and escape.

"Gullie." Toby shoved his shoulder. "Wake up. Come on, you Dark Fae fool."

Gulliver groaned as he lifted his head. There was a pain in his neck that hadn't been there before he fell asleep, but they weren't moving. "Another stop?" he asked.

Toby shook his head, peering out the window. "I think we're there."

"Thank the magic," he whispered, reaching down to zip up his bag. "Mrs. Merrick told me to look for a yellow car when we got here. Apparently, they'll let us use plastic money and take us to the address Tia gave us."

Toby didn't respond as he looped his bag over his shoulder and started toward the door. After so many hours cooped up with these humans, they didn't want to stay any longer than they had to.

Outside, there were more buses than they'd even seen in

Ohio. Some coming, others going. It was a mess of traffic that sent Gulliver's nerves into overdrive.

Why did humans insist on such loud, smelly machines? There was something to be said for a good steed and a quiet mountain pass. Even the Eldurian desert was better than this.

Gulliver dodged people who didn't seem to be watching where they were going. He slammed into someone and bounced back against Toby.

The man scowled, yelling a word Gulliver had never heard before, and shoved past them.

"Rude." Toby glared after him.

"Let's just find a yellow car and get out of here." He didn't particularly relish the thought of getting into another one of their metal contraptions, but he didn't know how far of a walk it would be to the address they had.

"There." Toby pointed to a small car that was, in fact, bright yellow.

At least it would get them out of this mess. They hurried toward it, yanking open the back door and piling inside before shutting the door. Shoving the slip of paper with the address to the older woman sitting in front, Gulliver said, "Go here."

She hit the gas, jumping the car forward, and it bounced down the road, weaving in and out of cars at a slightly terrifying speed.

Gulliver cracked his knuckles and then tilted his head to the side, just trying to loosen up his body after so long on that bus. Toby stared out the window with a menacing look, like he wanted to tear down the entire city. Maybe he did. It was whatever was going on here that forced his presence, after all.

"Do you think I'm going to get to hurt anyone?" Toby asked suddenly.

Gulliver caught the woman looking at them in the rearview mirror, her eyes wide. "Why would you ask that?" he whispered.

He shrugged. "I just ... I think it might help."

Gulliver rubbed his eyes. This was why Tia kept Toby locked up in the palace for so long. She was afraid of letting him out. How much courage had it taken from her to let him go this time?

He wanted a fight, to take out his anger on someone.

"Please don't hurt me," the woman said, her knuckles going white where she gripped the steering wheel. "I have grandchildren. Eleven of them. And four children. A husband. People who will look for me if I go missing. My husband is probably already wondering where I am since I wasn't there to get him at the bus station."

Nothing she said made sense. Gulliver leaned forward between the seats, and she shied away from him. "Why would we hurt you? Is this about money?" He pulled the card out of his pocket. "You can take as much from this as you want."

"Money?" A tear slipped down her cheek. "I don't need money. I just want to return to my family."

Gulliver and Toby shared a confused look.

"Is there something keeping you from your family?" Whatever Toby had been lately, he was still himself, still a protector, someone who always did what was right. He yanked Gulliver back so he could talk to the woman. "Do you need us to help you? Has someone hurt you?"

"Why are you doing this?" She used her shoulder to wipe her cheek. "You don't have to."

Gulliver stared at his hands, a realization hitting him. "Um, this is one of those taxi things, right?"

"No," she practically shouted. "This is my car! You got in and ordered me to go somewhere. I had no choice. I just wanted to pick up my husband. He's been gone for a month, visiting our son in Alabama, and I miss him."

"But ... but your car is yellow." Mrs. Merrick said to look for a yellow car.

"So?"

Oh, for magic's sake. They just abducted a woman from the bus station.

"What do we do?" Toby hissed.

"We have to let her go."

"Before we get there? Can't we just let her keep going?"

Gulliver punched his shoulder. "Absolutely not."

"No, you're right. Um, my lady, you can let us out anywhere."

She wasted no time swerving to a stop along the curb of an open-air market. Gulliver and Toby jumped out onto the sidewalk, grabbing their bags.

Gulliver stuck his head back in. "We're sorry for the trouble, lady. Please tell your husband he's lucky his wife has a yellow car that can drive him where he needs to go." He slammed the door, and she sped off so fast he had to jump out of the way.

"I don't think she liked us." He turned to Toby, who was inching away from two men.

"I bet I can tell you where you got your shoes," one of them said, waving a filthy rag in the air.

Gulliver looked down at the shoes Brea called sneakers. He didn't have a clue where Brea bought them. "You can?" he asked as the other man bent down to spray his feet with something shiny.

"I sure can." The other guy beamed a friendly smile. "Let me take a guess while my man here shines your shoes."

"Shines my shoes?" Gulliver looked down at his feet again. They might look better shiny, though he'd never considered that as something he looked for in shoes.

"We just need directions," Toby said, his voice gruff.

"Sure, sure." The friendly man bobbed his head. "I bet I can tell you where you got your shoes too."

"That doesn't seem necess—" Toby tried to move away from the shoe shiner man coming after him next.

"They're on your feet, bro." The man threw his head back and laughed.

"Now, that'll be twenty dollars for the shine and twenty for the line ... each," the second man said with a heavy accent.

Gulliver looked around them for some kind of line they wanted him to stand in. He shrugged. "Sounds reasonable." His eyes found a disapproving Toby. "If they say it's worth paying for, I believe them. Why would they lie? Let me ask you, sirs, does it look more ... normal to have shiny shoes?"

One grinned. "It does, young man. Now, you owe us eighty bucks."

Gulliver wondered what a buck was, hoping it was similar to a human dollar. "Do you take plastic money?" He reached for the card in his wallet.

A hand pushed his down, and he found himself looking into the eyes of someone who was very much not human. "Don't give them your credit card, you idiot." He turned to the men. "Get out of here before I call the cops." He shooed them away, and the two went running across the street toward some other tourists new to the city.

"Who are you?" Toby folded his arms across his chest, looking at the newcomer with suspicion.

The young man looked him over from head to toe, and Gulliver took that time to study him, from his umber-brown skin to the short-cropped black hair and golden haze in his eyes.

"My name is Xavier." He looked around, as if to make sure they were away from eavesdroppers. "Come with me." He took off toward an alleyway to the side of the marketplace, only stopping when the shadows hid them.

He blew out a breath and leaned against the brick wall. "Could you two scream fae any louder?" He shook his head. "There are people hunting us." His gaze found Gulliver's tail and sparked with curiosity, but he didn't ask questions. "You must be new to this city, but right now, it is the most dangerous place for fae. You should leave."

Toby shook his head. "We're here because it's dangerous."

Xavier stared at him for a moment before sighing. "I don't know you, so you're not my responsibility. Do whatever you'd like." He ripped the address out of Gulliver's hands. "Take this road here until it dead ends, turn left, and then make your first right. That's the street." He handed it back and started toward the parking lot, stopping at the mouth of the alley. "Try not to get yourselves killed."

Chapter Seven
SOPHIE-ANN

Hey Dad,

I picked up an extra shift today, so I won't be home till late. Don't wait up for me.

Sophie.

Coward. Sophie hung her head as she crept out of the house at an ungodly hour to avoid her father. She couldn't face him after what he'd done. The word execution had echoed through her mind all night long. That was what she'd witnessed. The execution of a man whose only crime was cheating on his wife. If he was fae, Sophie would eat her hat.

She pulled the brim of her baseball cap down low over her eyes. At this early hour, the Quarter was not a pleasant place to be. It stank of last night's revelry, and she avoided Bourbon Street altogether. For the moment, she shared the empty streets with the early workers, clean-up crews, and the last of the drunken tourists shuffling back to their hotels and B&Bs, wearing stupid grins and Mardi Gras beads when it wasn't even Mardi Gras.

She headed up to the city park on Decatur Street. It was her favorite place to sit on a blanket, soak up the sun, and read. She'd missed the sun when it went dark, and she wasn't alone. People had flocked to the city parks in droves, more than they ever had before.

But today, Sophie was restless, unable to get lost in the pages of her newest fantasy obsession. The fantasy worlds of her books had gotten all too real in recent years.

Ever since the world went dark when she was only eleven years old, her life had taken a drastic turn with her mother's death and the birth of her father's group, the Human Alliance For Survival.

It started in a few central locations across the world. The sun rose in the sky as it always did, but darkness seeped into the world, drowning out the sun's rays. Scientists attributed it to Global Warming, and others speculated that the sun was dying.

In the months after, the darkness continued to spread and daylight faded almost completely. All the major cities fell into chaos and anarchy. People thought it was the end of the world and quit their jobs to stay home with their families. Supplies were scarce and looters warred in the streets.

Sophie didn't remember much of the violence from that time because she'd stayed home with her mother, behind the safety of their walled property.

But the sun hadn't died. It was still warm and still hung like a black orb in the sky for all to see, but the light couldn't penetrate the perpetual night. The darkness had an effect on the mental health of the general population. Humans weren't meant to live without light. It wasn't natural.

That was when the first murmurings of otherworldly creatures began to arise. Some attributed the phenomenon to aliens, and others spoke of the fae. Creatures who lived in another realm that bordered the human world.

It became a witch hunt after that. So many were accused of being fae and were killed because of it. But they were out there. Sophie had seen it with her own eyes. Things that couldn't be explained. Her own mother died because of the fae and whatever they'd done to weaken the veil between the worlds.

Sophie's father knew more about them than anyone she'd ever known. He said their magic was responsible for the darkness seeping into the human world. It all started in a small town in Ohio. Then, other places fell into darkness. Like here in the Quarter, Central Park in New York, and a rural village in Ireland. From there, the darkness spread across the globe.

As the sun rose higher and the temperature became unbearable, Sophie picked up her blanket and her books and headed for the trolley stop on Saint Charles Avenue. The streetcars were Sophie's favorite thing about living in the city. Sometimes, she rode the them all day, letting the breeze cool her as she read her favorite books. From Esplanade Avenue all the way to the Garden District and back again, and again. At least until they kicked her off, and she moved to the Canal car or the Riverfront route.

Eventually, Sophie found herself on Canal heading toward the cemeteries, a huge draw for the tourists. She had to admit, the old cemeteries were interesting, with their above-ground mausoleums dating back centuries. The cities of the dead, the locals called them.

Sophie left her seat on the streetcar and made her way from Canal back to Saint Charles and, eventually, the Garden District and Lafayette Cemetery. Her feet moved along the familiar path through the gates and into the maze of tombs, avoiding the tourists and keeping her head down.

It was eerily quiet in the city of the dead. Like the noise of the Quarter couldn't reach past the iron gates to disturb those who were laid to rest here. But Sophie wasn't so sure her mother was at rest. Not considering how she died.

Sophie came to a stop at the Devereaux family tomb. Most of her family were entombed here, thanks to her great-grandparents, who had it built a few generations ago. Grandma Devereaux was the only one she'd actually known other than her mother. She liked to think they kept each other company so her mom wouldn't be lonely buried among her husband's people.

"Hi, Mama," Sophie whispered, laying her hand against the rough stone of the tomb. "I hope Gran is talking your ear off wherever you two are." A sad smile tugged at her mouth. "I miss you both." She set a bouquet of fresh flowers she'd picked from her mom's garden at the base of the tomb, tossing the old ones aside.

Standing, she plucked the ferns sprouting between the gray bricks and smoothed a hand over the crumbling facade. One day, she wanted to fix it up, but for the moment, it was enough that her grandmother's and mother's names were chiseled into the marble stone, just below the names of relatives she'd only heard of.

Sophie didn't remember much about her mother's funeral. Only the endless march through the Quarter and the music. She vividly remembered standing right here with her father, but she had no memory of what was said over her mother's grave. She'd been too lost inside her own grief and confusion to pay attention to mere words that didn't mean anything. Pretty words wouldn't bring her mom back.

"I don't know what to do, Mama." She closed her eyes, trying to remember the sound of her mother's voice, hoping she might recall some words of advice that would help her now. But nothing came to her. She'd forgotten too much about the woman who gave her life.

Forgotten too much about how she died.

All Sophie remembered was an otherworldly scream and a blast of power. Then, her mother lay dead on the ground beside her.

Sophie's father blamed the fae, and that was good enough for her. She hated the fae and everything they represented. Magic tore her family apart. Magic sent her world into darkness for months. And then, one day, the sun rose, the darkness faded, and everything went back to normal. On the surface.

But for Sophie Devereaux and those like her, everything had changed. Those who belonged to HAFS wanted revenge. They wanted to rid the human world of the fae and send them back to wherever they came from.

The only problem was they were really difficult to identify because they looked just like humans. To capture a fae, one had to see them use their magic. Magic they hid well.

People like Henry ... just didn't seem like fae to Sophie.

"I think Dad's carried it too far, Mama. And I don't know

how to stop him. I won't be with him much longer. Soon, I'll be with you and Gran. I'm afraid of what Dad will do once I'm gone." Sophie bowed her head, murmuring a trite prayer for the departed, hoping her passing would be a peaceful one that would end with her in the loving arms of her family.

She hated the fae. Hated everything they took from her, but she wasn't so sure she hated them so much she wanted to see them executed right in front of her. Not when she couldn't be sure they actually were guilty of harming humans with their magic.

"See you soon, Devereaux clan." She traced her fingertips over the column of names chiseled into the marble façade, letting her touch linger on the blank place where her name would soon join theirs before she turned to go.

It was time she stopped avoiding her father. The sun was high in the sky, and she'd wasted as much of the day as she could. If she was going to have to leave him behind, the least she could do was help him get past the vendetta he felt he owed his wife. Sophie wanted a better future for her father. He wasn't an old man, with the best years behind him. He deserved more than the early grave HAFS would give him.

Leaving Lafayette Cemetery and the Garden District behind, Sophie made her way home. She was too tired to stay out for the remainder of the day. And she had to face her father at some point.

The gunshot echoed in her mind as she walked down Esplanade Avenue toward the iron gates of her sanctuary. She wasn't sure she could ever get the image of her father pulling the trigger out of her mind. He'd never even hesitated or shown any remorse. This all started because a monster had taken her mother from them, but in the end, had her father turned into a different kind of monster?

"Sophie-Ann!" Claude Devereaux greeted her with a smile as she entered the courtyard. "Didn't expect you back so soon."

"I got off early." She hated herself for lying to her father. "They just needed some help with the morning rush." She refused to meet his gaze, shuffling over to the patio table to drop her pack and help him with the weeding.

"Thank you, honey. You sure you aren't too tired?" Concern filled his voice, and she hated it. Hated that she worried him so much.

She was tired from her jaunt through the city, but not too tired to help out. "I can do a little weeding." She knelt down on a knee pad and went to work on the box of lavender, sorting through the new growth for invasive weeds. Her mother had started the garden after they first moved into the house when Sophie was small. It was still hers. They just tended it for her. It was like having a living connection to her. As long as her herbs and flowers lived, a bit of her lived on too.

"We'll have leftover gumbo for dinner." He groaned as he got to his feet.

"Sounds good. I'll make some dirty rice to go with it." Sophie kept pulling weeds, moving on to the rest of the herb garden while her father chattered endlessly about HAFS news and plans for their next gathering.

Sophie offered up a second prayer for her dad, hoping he didn't have another meeting planned like the last one.

Chapter Eight
GULLIVER

"This city is kind of strange, even for humans." Gulliver peeked through the odd slatted blinds covering the windows into the streets below, where humans wandered around with bags, drinks, and gaudy-looking jewelry they wore around their necks. "We should go out this afternoon and explore. Tia said we'd have to search for fae in the area to get the story about what's happening to them."

"Have fun with that." Toby rolled over on the bed in the strange room to stare at the corner.

The room had two beds, and it reminded Gulliver of the inn he'd once stayed in with his father in the human realm. That was in a place called Ireland. But this building looked nothing like an inn. And the room was larger, with a couch and a television, along with something in the corner that looked a lot like a very small human kitchen with appliances he would likely break if he tried to use.

"You know, for a city that's supposed to be new, this place looks kind of grubby." Gulliver dropped the blinds and went to sit on his bed right beside Toby's. "I'd hate to see Old Orleans."

Toby continued to ignore him. After they arrived in the city the previous afternoon—once the nice lady they accidentally abducted let them out of her car—neither were up for any further excitement. But Toby still hadn't gotten out of bed, and the day was well underway. Dressed in his best human clothes, Gulliver was exceedingly aware of his role in this mission. There was no one to ask what they should do next. It was up to him. And he had no idea how to go about searching for fae villages within human cities.

"Want to go get some lunch?" Gulliver tried to tempt the sad prince with food as his own stomach growled. The innkeeper in the main house said something about a continent breakfast included with their stay, but nothing ever showed up at their door this morning, and Gulliver was starting to feel faint from lack of food. Most of what he'd brought with him was already gone after the long bus ride and the boring evening of watching Toby sleep.

"Bring me something when you return," Toby muttered, throwing a pillow over his head. "Wine. Bring me wine."

"When I return? Where am I going?"

"Go explore. Get the lay of the land. Just get out."

"You want me to go out there? By myself?" Gulliver's tail tried to flick out of his human jeans, but he'd bound it securely under his clothes so it didn't call any undue attention to them. Not that humans would see his tail either way, but he didn't want to take any chances. Humans were out there killing fae, and Gulliver had spent a lifetime defending his Dark Fae features to those who didn't understand them.

"Yeah, Gullie. Go find food, wine, and the fae villages, and then come back tonight with a plan. I'll be ready for action when you do."

"Really? Okay. I guess I could do some exploring just to get a feel for the city. You get some rest, Tobes." Gulliver gathered up his pack and checked his reflection in the mirror before he grabbed the room key that wasn't a key but a piece of plastic that looked too much like the plastic money Tia gave him. He was almost certain he would mix them up at the worst possible moment. "I hope you feel better soon." Gulliver glanced over his shoulder at his friend rolled up in the blankets like it was a freezing Iskalt morning. "I'm really going to need your help on this mission."

"Just bring me some wine, Gullie." Toby sighed. "That will help. For a while anyway."

Gulliver closed the door carefully behind him, flinching when the locks clicked with human magic. Stepping into the courtyard outside their room, he glanced around, unsure how to access the street. A pool of blue water sat at the center of the courtyard, and green ferns grew everywhere. A fountain tinkled at the edge of the walkway, and squashy moss grew all over the brick surrounding the fountain, where small orange fish swam around big green leaves that grew on top of the water.

An iron gate sat just beside the fountain, and the sounds of the city seemed to come from that direction.

"I sure hope you sent the right fae, Tia." Gulliver took a deep breath, tugged his hat down low over his eyes, and ducked through the gate onto the sidewalk. Tall trees with knobby trunks and weird, hair-like plants hanging from the branches towered over the street, casting the sidewalk in shadow.

Before he left, Tia taught him how to use the map on the human telephone she'd told him to take from the farmhouse. Her instructions were vague, though, and he still wasn't sure how to work it. Staring at the screen, everything he knew about human technology seemed to fall right out of his mind. But he started walking, hoping he could find his way back to the inn. He looked over his shoulder at the sign hanging over the iron gate he'd just stepped through. The Lamothe House. He committed it to memory, along with the street sign for Esplanade Avenue.

As he walked, Gulliver felt reasonably certain he'd never see the inn or Toby ever again. The city was vast, with street after street filled with similar-looking buildings and so many people. They were everywhere. Choosing at random, Gulliver headed down Royal Street, thinking he could easily remember that since he was here on a mission for his royal best friend.

"Royal Street to Esplanade Avenue," he muttered to himself. "Got it." He walked on for a long time, searching the faces of the people who passed him, wondering how he was supposed to find the fae.

Something very exciting seemed to be happening one street over. There was loud music, shouting, and general merriment, even at this early afternoon hour. And the people walking from that direction seemed to be about as drunk as anyone he'd ever seen. He wondered if this Bourbon Street might be a fae area. It would explain the strange behavior that seemed to be contained in just that location.

But today was about studying the city. Perhaps he would observe Bourbon Street later in the evening on his way back to the inn.

A strange building caught his attention, and Gulliver wandered across the narrow street, avoiding the honking cars that seemed like they didn't quite fit on the streets. Like the streets weren't built to accommodate them.

The old building wasn't any more intriguing than all the others, but the sign outside proclaimed it as the New Orleans Historic Voodoo Museum. A shrunken head hung from the sign, and all manner of odd things were on display in the windows.

"Excuse me?" Gulliver asked a lady in bright floral skirts standing outside the museum. "What is voodoo?"

"That is a loaded question, young sir." Her dark brown skin shimmered in the sunlight as she took a seat at the front of the museum. "Voodoo is part religion, part mysticism," she said in an oddly slow accented English Gulliver had never heard.

He took a step forward. "Mysticism?" That sounded like magic.

"The spirit world, boy. It is all around us." She waved her hands in the air. "We must keep the spirits happy, or bad things will happen." She leaned forward. "Come in for a tour and I'll show you all about the voodoo magic."

"Magic?" Gulliver smiled. "I'll return tomorrow with my friend. He'll want to see your shop too."

"Don't keep the spirits waiting too long, boy," she warned.

"I won't." Gulliver went on his way, down Royal Street, feeling a little better about this mission.

The day was growing hot, his clothes were sticking to his skin, and he was beyond hungry. Brea once said when Gulliver got good and hungry, he got grumpy as well. She said that was when he was hangry, which he was right this minute. And something wonderful caught his attention. A sweet fragrance that sent him down a side street to a place called the Vieux Carré Cafe.

"What deliciousness will you provide?" Gulliver took a seat at the outside patio under a canopy of shade trees, facing a big park and a cathedral. At the center of the park was a large statue of a man on a horse. In Gulliver's limited experience with humans, they didn't often ride horses. But even now, as he impatiently waited for someone to come bring him food, people rode by in horse-drawn carriages. It was such a familiar sight it made him a little homesick.

"Hi there, what can I get you?" A pretty girl with a shy smile came up to the table with a glass of ice water and a menu. Gulliver stared at her lovely blue hair for a moment, forgetting how to speak.

"Do you want a minute to look at the menu?" she asked.

"Hi. Um. Yes, what's that smell? I want whatever that is."

"Beignets?" She smiled. "First time in NOLA?" She scribbled something on a pad of paper.

"Um, yes." Gulliver wasn't sure what a nola was, but if the question was about his first time doing something human here, then it was an automatic yes.

"Would you like an iced coffee? It's a slightly sweet and creamy chicory blend we're famous for." She refused to look him in the eye, and her cheeks flushed pink under the scattering of freckles on her nose.

"Sure. Sounds good. But what's a Benny-ya?"

She laughed, the sound clear and sweet, like something she didn't do very often. "Beignets are like doughnuts dusted in powdered sugar. It's kind of the one thing about New Orleans that lives up to all the hype." She leaned in closer. "Just don't tell anyone I said that."

"I won't." Gulliver grinned. "I don't know anyone here." He shrugged. "What else is good?" He looked at the menu, but none of the words made much sense. "What's a Po Boy?"

"It's a street food thing with fried shrimp or oysters and coleslaw. It's probably the best thing on the menu, other than the beignets."

"Sounds good. I'll have the large."

"That's pretty big. You sure you don't want a half?"

"I'm pretty hangry."

The girl laughed again, her feet shuffling nervously as she scribbled on her pad. "Shrimp or oysters?"

"Uhhh, shrimp." Gulliver made a guess because he didn't know what either of those things were. The one thing he did know about human food was that if it was fried, it was probably delicious.

After the waitress left him with an awkward wave, he sat back and checked out his surroundings. Tugging on his hat, he shrank into his seat, trying not to look too conspicuous. He was used to getting odd looks wherever he went outside of Myrkur.

But no one gave him a second glance. They couldn't see his strange features. To all the other people dining outside the Vieux Carré Cafe, he was just another human having a late lunch.

Gulliver sat a little taller, lifting his chin. It was an odd feeling, blending into the crowd like everyone else. Even at home in Myrkur, he was the great Griffin O'Shea's adopted son. But when the other Dark Fae looked at him, it was with reverence and distance. He commanded respect he didn't feel like he'd earned, but few got close enough to really get to know him.

And everywhere else in the five kingdoms, Gulliver O'Shea was Queen Tierney's most trusted friend—and Dark Fae. He didn't know what it was like to just be himself among strangers

"I have your beignets." The waitress stumbled, and his food went flying across the table. "Oh no!" She set the basket down. Half of the little triangle pastries sat at the bottom of the basket and the other half lay in a scatter of white powder on the tablecloth in front of him. "I'm so sorry! I really have to stop doing that." She stomped her foot as nervous hands fluttered up to her face, and she cast a glance over her shoulder at a rather sour-looking blond woman watching from inside the restaurant. "I'll get you more." She reached for the beignets on the table.

"It's fine." Gulliver was quick to snatch them up and dump them back in the basket. "No harm done to the food." He stuck a finger in his mouth, and a burst of sweetness hit his tongue from the powdered sugar. It looked like Iskalt snow dusting the pastries.

"What's going on here?" The sour-looking woman came up to stand beside the flustered waitress.

"Nothing at all." Gulliver smiled. "I was just about to dive head first into these sweets."

"You spilled them everywhere ... again? Sophie, what am

I going to do with you?" She shook her head, reaching for the basket. "Please let me get you a fresh batch."

Gulliver clutched it to his chest. "I'm starving, and this food is perfectly fine, thank you."

"Well, at least let us bring you another batch. For the trouble."

"It's really no trouble." Gulliver stuffed a triangle into his mouth. "But if you want to bring me more of these, I'll eat them."

"Sophie." The woman snapped her fingers, and the girl all but ran back into the safety of the kitchen. "She's a bit of a klutz; I'm so sorry." The woman gathered up the tablecloth and moved his iced coffee and plates to another table.

"I don't know what a klutz is, but she's very kind and knowledgeable about the food. This is the best thing I've ever eaten, and that's saying something." Gulliver moved to the new table with the clean tablecloth, wondering what was wrong with the first one.

"I'll send over a new waitress to take care of you." She fussed over him like the poor girl had set him on fire.

"That's not necessary. I like Sophie just fine."

The girl in question rushed out with a fresh basket of sweets and whatever a Po Boy was.

"Sophie, you serve the sandwiches before the beignets," the insufferable woman groaned irritably. "I'm so sorry, sir." She took the sandwich from the tray. "Please take your time with your lunch, and then when you're ready, we'll bring out your beignets."

"No, don't bother." Gulliver took the platter with the huge sandwich and set it in front of him, nodding for Sophie to set the second basket of sweet things he couldn't pronounce right beside his plate. "I'm good here." He smiled at Sophie. "Honest."

"Thanks for your help, Vicky," the waitress said. "I think I've got it now."

"All right." She scowled at the girl. "I'm watching you," she mouthed as she walked away.

"Well, she's pleasant." Gulliver tucked a linen napkin into his shirt collar and went to work on the sandwich.

"I'm really sorry about all that." Sophie blushed, taking a step back. "Just, um, let me know if you need anything else."

"Thanks, Sophie." Gulliver gave her a shy smile. It was a rare thing when a pretty girl looked at him the way Sophie was staring at him right now. Like he was a handsome guy she wanted to impress.

"Enjoy your meal." She smiled again and shuffled away to check on her other customers.

As he tucked into his food, Gulliver thought he could get used to this. Sitting in a nice restaurant, blending in with the crowd, and flirting with cute waitresses who didn't think he was repulsive. Maybe spending some time in the human realm wouldn't be so bad.

Chapter Nine
SOPHIE-ANN

"Is that boy here again?" Vicky stepped up beside Sophie in the kitchen doorway to peer into the dining room. The man sat inside today.

"He's not a boy." Sophie saw a kind man who treated her like she mattered, even though she was only serving him food. Not to mention how completely adorable he was with soft brown hair that sat messily on his head and hung down into deep amber eyes. He had the build of a runner, long and lean, but not without muscle. So much different from the gym rat junkies that surrounded her in HAFS.

"Order up!" came from behind her.

She turned to grab the plate of beignets, a double order, and walked past Vicky.

The man smiled up at her. "Thank you."

She set the plate in front of him, unable to take her eyes from his. She didn't know anyone else who came in daily for beignets, let alone twice a day like yesterday. He didn't order anything else like that first day, except for a glass of water.

"You're welcome," she squeaked. Smooth, Sophie-Ann.

The door opened, and Gabe walked in. Her entire body tensed as he sat in her section, always hers, and waved her over. She stood frozen in place.

"Are you going to do your job?" Vicky called, nodding toward the newcomers.

Stiffly, she walked toward Gabe and pulled out her ordering pad. "What can I get you?"

"What?" He grinned up at her. "No hello? I thought we were friends, Soph."

"We are whatever my father decides," she muttered. It wasn't meant to be an acknowledgment, but he nodded.

"Good girl." He leaned in. "Your father wants to know if you've seen any suspicious customers in here this week. We're doing our typical rounds to New Orleans businesses, and I had the pleasure of being assigned to your lovely establishment."

"Don't you think I'd report something like that directly to my father?" HAFS kept an eye on the entire city, intimidating people into turning in anyone who rubbed them the wrong way.

Gabe lifted one brow. "Your father isn't so sure."

"You mean, you aren't. My father trusts me. Can you say the same?" Ever since her mother's death, her father refused to put his faith in anyone except his daughter.

Gabe's smile dropped. "You listen to me, you little—"

"Is there a problem here?" Her only other customer now stood behind her, drawn to his full height. In a fight, he'd be no match for Gabe, but having the stranger on her side calmed her.

"No." Gabe looked him up and down. "Not that it's any of your business, but I'm just having a chat with my girl here."

"She doesn't look like she's enjoying the chat."

"And?"

The man crossed his arms over his chest. "And that's a problem. I suggest you go get your pastries someplace else."

"Pastries." He narrowed his eyes. "You must be a tourist. Well, let me fill you in on how New Orleans works. I work for a group that runs this town. We don't appreciate tourists coming in and messing with our business. Stick to Bourbon Street."

Gabe stood. "I've lost my appetite, but Soph, you'll make this up to me." He stormed out, and she released a pent up breath.

She was watching the swinging door he'd disappeared through and didn't realize the man was still behind her until he spoke.

"Are you okay?"

A soft laugh escaped her. "I'm used to him." Pushing a hand through her short, blue-streaked hair, she turned and put on her best fake smile. "You shouldn't have stepped in like that." She walked past him toward the kitchen.

He followed. "Why not? You looked like you needed help."

"And you just help any stranger? That could get you killed, sir. Or at least hurt. I don't know where you're from, but this city is not what it appears on the surface. It's not just a fun jaunt to drink and party."

"I'm from Ohio."

That explained his naïveté. "Well, it's probably better for your health if you let people fight their own battles."

"Battles don't scare me. I've seen many of them in my lifetime."

She turned to face him, studying the earnestness in his expression. "What's your name?"

"Gulliver."

"What an odd name."

"Is that bad?"

One side of her mouth lifted into a half-smile. "No. It's just odd. I like it."

"You can call me Gullie."

There was something so honest, so rare in this man she couldn't help wanting to dive inside his mind, to see the world through his eyes. "How long are you in New Orleans?"

"I'm not sure. I'm here for work, and it could take a while."

"Then, you're going to want to stay clear of men like Gabe." She glanced toward the door. "And if you're going to eat beignets every day, I have two tips for you."

He leaned in. "I want to hear these ... tips."

He did. She could see it in his curious eyes. Gullie wanted to listen to her, to take in her words. It was so rare in her world that she couldn't help smiling. "First, take up running."

"Will they give me extra running speed?"

She laughed. "You're funny."

Confusion flashed across his face, but he shook it off. "And the second?"

She pulled a napkin out of her apron, stepping closer to wipe his cheek. "Learn to clean the powdered sugar off your face."

It was only when his breath hitched that she realized just how much she'd invaded his space and retreated, handing him the napkin. "I should get back to work."

He continued cleaning his face. "Yes, I should go get my roommate out of bed." He gave her a small bow. "It was a pleasure seeing you today, Sophie."

She was still smiling long after he was gone. There was only one thing she knew about this strange man. He'd return tomorrow. She was sure of it.

The cafe was packed by the time Sophie clocked in.

"You're late." Vicky held a tray with one hand, brushing past Sophie to set plates on a nearby table before returning.

"I know. I'm sorry. Today was another lecture from my dad about wasting my potential." That was the line she gave everyone. In truth, it had taken her too long to dress, to make it down the stairs. The days were getting worse. Soon, she wondered if she'd even be able to get out of bed. Dying was strange. At first, the news was a shock. Then, it just became another part of life. The weakness normalized until she could hardly remember a time before.

Sophie's vision swam as she looked out at the full tables. Vicky thought she was the biggest klutz on the planet when in reality, dizziness hit her at random times.

If her father wasn't so insistent that she was fine and the

job was good practice for her future, she wouldn't be working now.

Trying to hide her ragged breathing, she headed into the dining room to where two tables of hers had just seated themselves. Vicky took the outdoor tables today, and for that, she was grateful. The sun was not a welcome sensation on her skin right now.

The first table was a family of four, with two adorable kids who were probably bored on a family trip to New Orleans. Sure, there were some things for kids to do, but it was more of an adult vacation spot. "Hi, I'm Sophie, and I'll be your waitress today. Can I start you with something to drink?"

The tiny red-headed girl couldn't have been more than five. She waved up at Sophie, a giant smile on her face. Her brother, looking equally as young, gave her a shy smile and said, "You're pretty. I like your hair."

Sophie laughed. "Why thank you, sir. I hope you're enjoying your stay here in New Orleans."

"Oh, yes," the mother gushed. "This city is beautiful. So much culture and history. It must be amazing to live here."

Sophie didn't know any different from this city, with its pothole-filled streets in front of incredible multi-million-dollar homes with more charm than many places had in their entire towns. Not to mention the melding of cultures, the mysticism. She wanted to see more of the world, but this was home. "It is."

She pictured this family returning to their suburban lives, where the kids played soccer and came home to a house that looked just like all the others. They were probably happy, all their problems small.

The father leaned in, dropping his voice. "We're actually here for a reason. Renauld over at the daiquiri place told us we might be able to find the information here."

"Sure." Tourists asking questions about where to find things in the city wasn't anything new. "Are you looking for some kind of tour? There's a great one that'll take you out to where The Battle of New Orleans took place, and—"

"Actually, have you heard of the Human Alliance For Survival?"

Her heart sank, and she suddenly saw the family through new eyes. Kids who'd grow up with the same kind of hate their parents harbored, parents so obsessed with finding the "others" that they'd let horrible injustices slide right on by. "Never heard of it," she lied.

"Really?" The mother's smile dropped. "That's disappointing. We come from the Dallas chapter and were hoping to attend a meeting while we're here."

The meetings didn't happen on a regular schedule. Members usually received a coded text only hours before they had to be there. So, even if Sophie wanted this family to get into a local meeting, she wouldn't have the information they needed. "I'm sorry. I can't help you."

The father nodded. "Well, in that case, we'll take four orders of beignets, two coffees, and two apple juices."

Sophie nodded, her movements rigid.

She turned to head back toward the kitchen when someone else caught her eye. A wave of dizziness came over her, tilting the world on its side. She dropped the order pad, the pen bouncing off the tile. Strong hands gripped her, holding her upright.

"Sophie." Gulliver sounded panicked. "Are you okay?"

She shook herself, the spinning fading away as she regained her strength. "Yes. I'm fine." Righting herself, she stepped away. "I think I just need some water."

"I have some. I haven't touched it yet." He led her to his table and forced her to sit, sliding the cold, sweating glass across to her. It left a slick of water behind.

"I should really be working." She sipped the water, wishing this wasn't so difficult.

"No. Drink more."

"Sophie." Vicky stomped toward them, making a scene. Customers turned to stare. "What do you think you're doing?"

"She needed a moment." Gulliver's brows drew together.

"She has work to do. Have you put your last table's order in?"

"I'll do it." Gulliver stood, bending to pick up the order pad. He didn't wait for permission before marching to the kitchen, where he slapped the ticket on the counter. When he returned a moment later, he offered Vicky a smile. "They said the order will be right up. I'm not sure how high up it will be, but I assumed you could figure it out."

Sophie hid a laugh behind her hand. She'd never met anyone who could make a joke out of pretty much anything and not sound like they were trying too hard. For Gullie, the lightness came naturally, like he was born to it.

Vicky stared hard at them both. "The trash needs taken out." She stormed away, leaving Sophie and Gullie staring at each other. Neither could help laughing.

"I should go before she murders me." She stood.

Gulliver's eyes widened. "That seems like an extreme punishment."

She suppressed a laugh, trying to play along. "There are worse ones."

Worry lined his face, and for a moment, she thought it might be real. But he had to know she was joking, right?

Heading back to the kitchen, she lifted the half-full trash bag out of the can. It didn't need to be taken out, but whatever Vicky wanted, Vicky got. She tied it shut and pushed through the door to the alleyway out back.

The moment it shut behind her, two hands grabbed her, shoving her face-first against the wall. The bag hit the ground and split, sending waste across the pavement.

"Ow, let me go. Do you know who my father is?"

Abduction was a constant risk when her father was enemy number one of the fae, but she knew how to protect herself. Kicking a foot out, all she felt was air.

Someone laughed. "I know all your tricks, princess." Gabe turned her around to face him. "Don't worry, honey. Your father is the one who wants to see you." He pressed a rough kiss to her lips, and she bit him.

He leaned away with a smile, his finger gingerly touching where she'd drawn blood. "I so very much enjoy when he sends us to retrieve you."

"And one day, I will very much enjoy wringing your neck."

More laughter and she realized just how many of her father's men were there. Whatever he wanted couldn't be good.

Chapter Ten
GULLIVER

Toby wasn't there. The one time Gulliver needed him was the one time he'd decided to go into the city alone.

He hadn't seen Sophie in days. She'd left to take the garbage out and never returned. When he'd gone to look for her, the trash lay scattered in the alley and there was no sign of the waitress.

He didn't know this city, didn't know this girl or what she could possibly be involved in, but he wanted to find her, to help her if he could. It was what his father would do.

"I wish you were here right now, Dad." He sat on his bed and rested his head in his hands. They'd been in the city for a week now and had no signs of this supposed fae-hunting group or even the fae they were after.

Well, except for the one who threatened them their first day. He'd never felt more alone in his life, and yet, he wasn't alone here.

"Toby," he growled. "You blasted idiot. You better be easy to find." He was done with Toby's moping. Done with his grief. Yes, the man he loved was dead, but a lot more fae could die if the two of them didn't get their act together.

He had to find him.

Tearing from the room, he thundered down the stairs and out into the courtyard. Once he reached the street, he tried to think where Toby would go. "Think, Gullie," he whispered to himself. Somewhere that reminded him of home. That could be a lot of places. There were so many magic shops in this city, and none of them were for real magic. At least, the kind of magic he was used to.

Like him, Toby didn't have much magic. Except for the portals. He wouldn't have left, would he? The old Toby wouldn't, but he wasn't the same fae.

No. Gulliver had to believe he was still here. He wandered the streets near the inn for a while before it hit him. Magic. Turning around, he headed toward the voodoo shop he'd come across on his first day of exploring. He still wasn't sure what voodoo was, but the owner claimed it was mystical, a kind of magic. Maybe it really was.

He was almost there when he saw him. Toby sat on the curb, his knees bent and elbows resting on his thighs. His head hung between his hands. He looked defeated.

"Are you drunk?" Gulliver asked, wishing he could take it back the moment the words left his mouth.

Toby lifted his head and glared up at him. "I should be."

Gulliver hesitated a moment before sitting next to him. "No, you shouldn't. It's time to face the world, Tobes."

"I know." He rubbed a hand across his face. "What did

Tia think sending the two of us on such an important mission?"

"Probably that we'd never failed her, and we aren't about to start now."

"I've failed her for months."

"Can we stop with the pity party?" Normally, Gulliver had endless patience. It came from being Tierney's best friend. Sort of a requirement of the job. But right now, he was too worried about where a certain waitress could be.

"I went looking for the fae, thinking it would make me feel like I was home. The locals say this place is magic." He gestured back at the voodoo shop. "But I didn't feel any."

"Maybe it's their kind of magic."

He shrugged. "Doesn't help us."

They fell into silence for a long moment before Gulliver sighed. "I lost my waitress."

"You ... what? Your waitress?"

"Not mine, exactly. But she's been serving me pastries all week, and now she's not. I thought humans went to their jobs every day. They live for them. But I keep going back and she's not there."

"Maybe she—" His words cut off as the ground below them shook and fire rent the air only a few blocks away.

Both fae jumped to their feet.

"Was that ..." Toby started.

"An explosion." Gulliver tugged on his arm. "Come on." They sprinted down the street, where humans rushed out of buildings to see the smoke blackening the sky for themselves.

They followed the flow of the crowd until they reached a blazing row of buildings right in the heart of New Orleans.

"What do you think happened?" Gulliver overhead a human ask another.

The other shrugged. "Most likely witches."

"It wasn't witches," a low voice said as Xavier stepped up between Gulliver and Toby. "Do nothing sudden. Come with me." They'd only met the fae once when he issued a warning to them, yet he was one of them, and Gulliver followed him without question.

"How do you know it wasn't witches?" Toby asked.

"Because human witches do not have what you or I think of as magic. They are more spiritual than actually magical. Keep up." He increased his pace until they reached the rear of the crowd and kept going onto an empty street.

"Humans did this." Xavier looked behind them to make sure they weren't followed.

"What?" Gulliver didn't know if he could believe that. "Why would humans blow up their own buildings?"

"You obviously know nothing of human history." He turned sharply to climb up three steps and knocked twice on the door of a narrow blue house. "It's Xavier."

An elderly woman opened the door. "It was the tourist center, wasn't it?" She stepped away from the door to let them in.

Xavier nodded, removing his hat. "Found two strays there and figured I should get them away from the crowd." He gestured to Toby and Gulliver. "Take your shoes off and come in."

Once inside, Gulliver looked around the small house. The door led straight into a bedroom and then a long sitting room. Beyond that was a tiny kitchen at the back. It was a strange house with barely any furniture.

"You're safe here," Xavier said. "We use this house when any of us need to escape from the city. May is a human friend."

May must have been the woman who let them in.

"There are humans who befriend the fae here?" Gulliver asked.

"Of course there are. Not all humans want to see us eradicated." He dropped onto the settee.

Toby stayed in the doorway. "You mentioned a tourist center."

"The fae run many businesses in this town. One of them was a place for tourists to get information about activities. We used it to connect visiting fae with our communities. Secrecy is important here, so we must be careful."

May walked in with three mugs. "Tea?"

"Thank you." Xavier took one, so the others followed suit. He took a sip before setting it on the table next to him. "Now, tell me why you're both here."

Gulliver and Toby shared a look, neither wanting to answer. Would this man laugh in their faces if he knew the truth? Try to stop them from investigating?

Xavier sighed. "I know you're not from New Orleans. No fae lives in this city without us knowing about it. Are you from the New York community?" He paused, dark fingers running along his solid jaw. "No. Midwest."

"I don't know where that is," Gulliver said. "But what are we doing here? Shouldn't we be out there helping?"

"How? By alerting HAFS to your presence? No." He cocked his head. "You really don't know anything about us, do you?"

Toby grunted. "You already decided we aren't from here. How would we?"

"Interesting." He leaned back, reached for what Brea called a remote, and turned on the television. A human appeared in front of the explosion site with the same claim they'd heard.

Witches.

"We suspect the recent bombings are from the same forces that turned our world dark so many years ago. It may all be happening again."

"The mainstream media always blames witches or science." Xavier kicked his feet up onto the table. "Before the darkness, no one would have said witches even existed. But now, it's a convenient way to get out of blaming their own. Many of the humans agree with what this terrorist group is doing; they just won't say it."

He pointed at the screen. "Do you see why you shouldn't be here if you do not know this city? These humans may not be able to see your eyes or that tail you're trying to hide—something I've never seen before—but they will sniff you out with their dying breath."

"Why do they care so much?" Gulliver didn't know many humans. There was Myles and Alona, though she was raised as fae. A few people in Ohio. Each of them was kind, welcoming.

Xavier sighed. "Because they fear us, what we can do. Most of us don't ..." He stopped, clamping his lips shut.

"Don't what?"

"Nothing. It's not important. Just know, to stay alive here, you must fit in."

The door banged open and two women walked in. They

were tall, taller than any man here. The first had raging emerald eyes, pointed ears, and an untouchable aura. The second was more delicate. Gulliver's gaze traveled from her long, lithe limbs with her umber skin, beautiful hazel eyes, and bright white wings stretching out behind her.

The first one kicked the door shut and shoved Toby out of the way to walk into the room, her eyes finding Xavier.

He stood. "How many?"

"Four." The second folded her wings around her like a shield, but her tears were still visibly sparkling on her smooth cheeks. "Including Tina and Mathew."

Xavier cursed. "They weren't even fae." He kicked the table, and it overturned, sending his tea spilling across the floor as the mug shattered. A roar escaped his throat. "Why didn't we have a warning?"

"We did," the winged woman said. "That's why it wasn't worse. There was a meeting going on, some of our elders gathering to discuss possibly leaving New Orleans."

"No." Xavier pinned her with a glare. "We will not abandon this city. It belongs to us as much as them." He pinched the bridge of his nose. "At least most of the fae got out."

Gulliver couldn't hold his questions in any longer. "Are there more Dark Fae living in the human realm?"

The woman wiped the tears from her face. "Dark Fae?"

"You know ... from Myrkur ..."

"I don't know what you're talking about. I'm from Louisiana. My family has been here for generations. And now, they're trying to drive us out."

"But the wings ..."

"Gullie," Toby hissed. "Not the time."

There were so many things he wanted to know. How big was this community they spoke of? Did none of them know anything of the fae realm? And just how many communities of fae were there?

"We have to find a way to fight back." Xavier bent to where May had started cleaning up his mess and took the towel from her to do it himself, absently wiping up the tea.

As he watched Xavier, Gulliver couldn't help thinking about the waitress who spilled food every time he was at the cafe. "There's a girl," he blurted. "Maybe you all can help me find her."

"Not this again," Toby groaned.

All three of the other fae looked at Gulliver.

The first one spoke, her eyes returning to a natural green. "Who are you?"

"Strays." Xavier waved off the question. "Can't have idiots getting themselves killed in our city."

She pursed her lips. "I'm Sasha. This is Amandine." She gestured to the winged fae.

"Gulliver and Toby." He pointed to himself then to Toby.

Sasha nodded. "Now, what's this about a missing girl?"

He went into the story, much to Toby's chagrin, of meeting her and returning to the cafe. They listened, and he appreciated that because he knew they'd just lost friends, that there were more important things going on than a single missing woman.

He didn't notice the suspicion clouding Amandine's face until she asked, "And the waitress's name?"

"Sophie."

"And she works at the Vieux Carré Cafe?"

"Yes! You know her? If you could please—" His words were cut off when each woman grabbed an arm and dragged him toward the front door. "What's going on?"

Amandine opened the door, shoving him down the steps. He hit the cracked sidewalk and pain shot through his shoulder. Toby landed beside him.

When Gulliver looked up, only Xavier stood in the doorway. "Sophie-Ann Devereaux is not a woman you want to find." He tossed their shoes down and slammed the door.

Pedestrians stepped over them as more continued down the road toward the fire. Gulliver pushed himself up, trying to catch his breath. "You okay, Tobes?"

Toby lay on his back, staring up at the gray sky. "That was kind of fun."

Gulliver extended a hand down and pulled him to his feet. "You're deranged."

He shrugged. "At least we gained a valuable piece of information."

"And what's that?" Gulliver slipped his shoes back onto his feet.

"Your waitress. If they hate her so much they'd abandon their own, she might be the key."

"The key to what?"

"Finishing this mission and returning home."

He looked sideways at Toby, glad he wasn't in this alone. Tia had known what she was doing sending the both of them. He clapped a hand on Toby's shoulder. "So, we find her?"

"Absolutely. Then, we come up with a plan."

Chapter Eleven

SOPHIE-ANN

"I'm sorry, Dad." Sophie lifted a trembling hand to her clammy brow, ignoring Gabe and his idiot friends standing in the living room behind her. "I'm not feeling very well."

Her father rushed to her side, despite the full house of HAFS members in a seemingly celebratory mood. "You look tired." He studied her face, frowning at the dark circles under her eyes. "Go upstairs and have a lie down. We'll call you back for the meeting in a bit."

"She's fine, Claude," Gabe was quick to add. "She's still mad we picked her up from work early."

"Dragged me away from my job in the middle of a shift is more like it," Sophie snapped, feeling lightheaded. "And then kept me practically locked up here for days to supposedly keep me safe. From what, I still don't know. I'll be lucky if I even have a job when I go back."

"I'll put in a call to Ben and have him smooth things over

with Vicky. You shouldn't let her push you around anyway. She's just the manager."

"And my boss."

"But Ben signs your paychecks. Remember that."

"Whatever." Her dad was never going to get what it was like working with Vicky. Every time he went to Ben about things like this, Vicky made her life miserable. More miserable than usual. "Just let me handle things with my boss."

"All right." He gave her a gentle shove toward the stairs that led to her bedroom. "Get some rest, sweetheart."

The stairs up to her bedroom might as well have been a mountain, but she took each one slowly, hauling herself up using the rail for support. Sophie's bedroom had once been used as a choir loft when the house was a chapel. The long, narrow room was now closed off and housed her bedroom, bathroom, and walk-in closet.

By the time she reached the safety of her bedroom, Sophie was sweating and shaking.

She collapsed onto her bed, the room spinning as she closed her eyes to the dulcet tones of Gabe's annoying voice.

"You coddle her too much, Claude," Gabe said, not bothering to lower his voice. If she could hear him, then everyone in the house could. Just what she needed, everyone knowing her business. "She's never going to be ready to lead the cause until someone rips her out of that shell she hides in."

Sophie rolled over, trying to shut out the din of too many people stuffed into the small house.

"You don't know what you're talking about, Gabe." Her father's deep voice was as soothing as it had always been. "You leave my daughter to me." Only her dad knew the truth. She wouldn't be around long enough to lead anyone.

"Score one for Dad." Sophie sighed as she pulled a blanket over her, kicked off her shoes, and fell asleep in an instant.

Being chronically ill and trying to act like everyone else was the most exhausting thing Sophie-Ann Devereux had ever done.

"Wake up, Sleeping Beauty." A gentle voice pulled Sophie from a deep sleep filled with dreams of warm amber eyes and a kind smile covered in powdered sugar.

"Mmm?" she groaned, eager to get back to her dreams. Dreams were the one place where she was never tired or in pain.

"Come on, Soph, we've got people waiting for us downstairs." Warm breath brushed against her ear, and her eyes snapped open.

"You better not be in my bed." She wanted to roll away from him the second she realized Gabe was the one breathing on her, but it would take her a few minutes to get out of bed and on her feet.

"We're having a celebration, and you've been up here for hours being lazy." Gabe moved to sit on the edge of the bed. "Go put on your best dress."

"My best—and only—dress is for funerals, which we'll all be going to if you don't get out of my room right now." Sophie dragged herself to the opposite side of the bed. "And if you knew me at all, you'd know I don't do dresses."

"Well, put on something decent at least and come down.

Everyone's waiting for you. And do something with your hair. You know I prefer it when you wear it down."

"Get out now and I might think about leaving this room." She settled her feet on the floor and moved to sit up, the room spinning like a top, leaving her nauseated. She reached out to clutch the edge of her dresser for support. The last thing she wanted to do was socialize with HAFS. Not after what happened at the last meeting.

She'd supported her father in the beginning when he first created this sector of HAFS. Too many people had chosen to ignore the unnatural darkness the fae brought to their world, choosing to believe the fake news that claimed it was witches or some solar flare phenomenon that could be explained away with science. With fae creatures hiding among the humans, and no way to identify them until it was too late, someone had to do something to spread awareness. That was where she thought HAFS was the most beneficial. But sometimes, she wondered if her father had taken things too far from the group's roots.

After witnessing an execution, where she'd done nothing to help that poor man, she hated herself for her involvement.

"Make it quick, and do something about the shadows under your eyes too. You're too young to be looking so rough after half a shift waiting tables." Gabe moved to stand by the door. "We might need to get you a gym membership to work on your stamina."

"Get out," Sophie said, her voice cracking on the words. "There is no *we* here."

"Don't be like that, Soph." He turned to her with a wide grin. "Especially not when your father has just given his permission for us to marry." He leaned against the doorframe, his grin widening into a leer.

"Not possible." Sophie shook her head. There was no way her father would agree to that. What was the point in her marrying anyone when she was dying? "He wouldn't do that to me." Not when he knew how much she loathed Gabe.

"It's a done deal." Gabe crossed the room to her closet, rummaging through her things, pulling out blouses and pants she hadn't worn in ages. "The recent attack on the fae in the Quarter was my doing. I led a team of HAFS on your father's orders. It was my win." He tossed the clothes onto the bed where she sat, unable to speak. "You're my prize."

"You're disgusting," Sophie croaked, the words lodging in her throat.

Gabe just laughed at her. "Come down. Now. We're celebrating our success, and Claude wants to announce our engagement as soon as you make an entrance." He turned to go. "Oh, and just so you know, once we're married, I won't tolerate this nonsense. You're a grown woman, Soph. You shouldn't be taking naps in the middle of the day. Claude coddles you, but I won't."

"Get out!" Sophie threw a pillow at him.

The door closed behind him, but his laughter echoed down the stairs.

Sophie sat shaking on the edge of her bed. How could her father even discuss such a thing without her? Let alone agree to it. She moved woodenly, pulling on a pair of dark jeans and a clean t-shirt. Running a brush through her hair, she twisted it up into a neat bun. No way was she wearing it down for Gabe.

As she made her way downstairs, her movements went

from wooden and slow to deliberate and fueled by rage. The revelry below had reached top volume in celebration over the deaths of many. She paused on the stairs. They were offering up congratulatory toasts to the demise of the fae. A tragedy that had likely killed more humans than non.

Sophie would be the first to say the fae needed to be dealt with. Too many people had died from their magic. People like her mother. But this ... She couldn't celebrate when innocent humans were hurt. She wanted no part of HAFS if that was the direction they were going.

"Sophie-Ann!" her father called above the noisy din of the crowd. The largest part of their home, the living room, used to be the sanctuary when the building once served as a chapel. The ceiling towered overhead, with exposed beams and trusses. A huge wall of windows and French doors stood open, overlooking the courtyard and letting in the evening light and a cool breeze.

She stepped into the room, and there were HAFS members standing shoulder to shoulder, spilling out into the courtyard.

"Dad, we need to talk." She wound through the crowd to where he was holding court at the dining room table, a large slab of natural wood still edged with the bark from the tree it came from. Her father had made it himself when she was young. Back when he had a successful woodworking business that had failed in the years after her mother's death. Now, he worked construction to pay the bills.

"We're celebrating, sweetheart." His smile hit a chord in her heart. He was clearly drunk, but that was a real smile. One she rarely saw anymore. "Grab a beer from the fridge."

"You know I can't drink." She moved to sit beside him

after one of his men stood to offer her the seat. "It interferes with my medication."

"Right." He nodded, giving her that look that said he didn't want to talk about her illness. He'd worked hard to keep her condition from the HAFS community. She was supposed to be the one to take over for him when he retired, but they both knew she wouldn't be here for that. He would have to choose a successor from among his loyal followers.

"What are we celebrating?" she asked, though she knew.

"To the success of HAFS and our most recent victory over the fae."

"And what of the human deaths?" She gave her father a kick under the table. "What of them?"

"Unfortunate casualties of war," Gabe answered, coming to stand behind her.

"Should we not be mourning the loss of our own? Perhaps discuss ways we can avoid such tragedies in the future?"

"Don't bring us down, Soph." Gabe brushed a hand down her shoulder, squeezing harder than necessary. Hard enough to leave a bruise, though she tended to bruise easily because of her illness.

She was getting strange looks from those across the room, and she realized she was never going to get through to them. They were hungry for blood. Fae blood. And they didn't care who got in the way.

A chair scraped against the floor, and all the color drained from her face as her father stood up raising his beer for a toast. "I have an announcement to make." He turned to his daughter. "Sophie-Ann, this includes you. Come stand with me, sweetheart."

She shook her head. "We have to talk. Now." She stared down at her lap, unable to meet her father's eyes. He couldn't be doing this. He couldn't be so callous.

Gabe took her by the arm and pulled her up from the chair. "Come on, Soph. Don't ruin this," he whispered in her ear as he shoved something onto her finger, the thin metal scraping her skin.

There was nothing she could do. She glared at her father as he addressed his people.

"Ladies and gents." He tapped his bottle against the edge of the table to get everyone's attention. "I have a happy announcement to make."

"You can't do this," Sophie hissed under her breath.

Her father ignored her, refusing to meet her gaze as he lifted his beer bottle, the light shining through the amber glass. "I'm pleased to announce that Gabe came to me earlier tonight and asked for my daughter's hand in marriage." He paused for the applause and cheers that swept through the room.

Gabe grinned and laughed as those closest to him slapped him on the back.

"It was a difficult decision." Her father sighed. "Sophie-Ann is precious to me. But Gabe has been the son I never had, so it does my heart proud to be able to say I have given them my blessing."

More cheers and catcalls echoed around her, and no one seemed to notice the horrified, betrayed look on her face as she watched her father make decisions for her.

"To the engagement of my daughter, Sophie-Ann Deveraux, to my right-hand man, Gabriel Christoph—the man of the hour." Her father beamed a smile as Gabe wrapped an arm around her shoulders. "Congratulations. I wish you both great happiness in your lives together."

"Hear, hear!"

"Try to look happy, Soph." Gabe leaned in to press his head against hers as people started taking pictures and asking to see the ring.

Sophie stood, stunned in a sea of smiling faces, everyone celebrating her engagement when no one had even bothered to ask her if it was what she wanted.

"No," she whispered, shaking her head. "No!" she shouted louder and louder still, until the room grew silent. "I'm *dying*! I can't get married. Certainly not to you." She tugged the cheap ring off her finger and threw it at Gabe before she turned to her father. "How could you?" She shoved her way through the crowd, desperate for a moment alone and a breath of fresh air. She ran across the courtyard and through the iron gates onto the sidewalk, and she didn't stop running until she couldn't take another step. She collapsed onto a park bench near the trolley station, letting the tears break free.

Chapter Twelve
GULLIVER

Sophie set the basket of pastries in front of Gulliver, and he saw the bruises along a finger of her left hand. Without thinking, he grabbed her hand, startling her.

"Sorry, I um ..." He fumbled over his words. "Didn't mean to scare you. What happened to your hand?" His eyes traveled up the length of her arm, where another bruise peeked out from under her t-shirt sleeve. It looked suspiciously like a thumbprint. Gulliver couldn't imagine why anyone would want to hurt Sophie. She was so nice. And pretty. And a thousand other things he liked about her.

"I hope the other guy looks worse." He tried to pull a smile out of her. He loved it when she smiled at him for no reason other than she thought he'd said something funny. But Sophie had seemed odd over the last few days. She'd come back to work like she hadn't been abducted from the alley behind the café and refused to give any sort of explanation, only retreating into herself if Gulliver tried to ask.

The light had gone out of her eyes. and she moved lifelessly from one table to the next, giving little notice to the people who came and went throughout her shift. All except him. She still seemed to take notice whenever Gulliver sat down at his regular table.

"Oh, it's nothing." Her hands fluttered awkwardly as she fumbled with the notepad she used to take orders. "I bruise easily." She brushed a short lock of her odd blue hair out of her face.

Gulliver stared at her hair. He never knew humans could have such things as blue hair, but he really liked it.

"Can I get you anything else?" She refused to meet his gaze.

"I saw him. That man who was bothering you the other day. He was on the feletision."

A smile tugged at her mouth, and Gulliver eagerly awaited seeing it light her eyes. No doubt he'd said something stupid again.

"You mean the television?"

"Oh, right. I always say stuff wrong by accident." Gulliver dropped his gaze down to the basket of heavenly sweets that awaited him. But for once, he was more interested in the girl than the food she'd brought him. "He doesn't seem like a very nice guy."

"He's not." She sighed. "But I can handle him. My father's another matter."

"Sophie! Stop flirting with customers and get back to work!" Vicky rang the buzzer that let the servers know orders were backed up.

Sophie's pale face flushed a delicate shade of pink.

"Gotta get back to work." She shuffled away, looking both weary and embarrassed at the same time.

Gulliver went back to his beignets and iced coffee, but he kept an eye on Sophie as she moved around the restaurant. The cafe was busier today than usual, and he didn't get a chance to talk to her again before he finished his snack. But something caught his eye on a nearby table after the group of humans left talking loudly.

"That attack was the first of many." A thin man with a weak chin tossed a bundle of paper onto the table. "I just hope that the HAFS group takes them all out. The fae don't belong in our world."

"They don't, but I just don't like to see any humans getting hurt. Those boys from HAFS could have been more careful with human lives." A petite woman with dark hair and kind eyes followed the man from the cafe.

"What's a HAFS?" Gulliver muttered as he slipped out of his seat and retrieved the rolled-up papers from the empty table and took it back to his own. Sinking down in his seat, Gulliver stared at the familiar face on the cover of what he believed was a human thing called a newspaper. The picture staring back at him was the same one he'd seen on the big screen thing Tia called a TV. Toby had figured out how to turn it on, but they didn't know how to look for Netflix like they had at the farmhouse, so it stayed on the same channel. It was always the news. Boring and tedious. Why anyone wanted to watch that was beyond him.

"Gabriel Christoph," he read the name under the picture. Hadn't Sophie called him Gabe?

Gulliver bent to read the article.

Gabriel Christoph and several unknown members of the

local New Orleans sector of HAFS, the Human Alliance For Survival, were suspects in the explosion that left the French Quarter reeling only days ago.

The explosion, thought to be an act of terrorism against the suspected fae colonies within the human realm, left dozens injured and eighteen dead. HAFS members across the country believe magical creatures known as fae are responsible for the darkness that threatened our world over a decade ago, yet there is little evidence to corroborate that myth.

The local HAFS leader, Claude Devereaux, made the following statement just after the explosion:

"It is regrettable that human lives were lost in such a terrible tragedy. Rather than focusing the investigation against the innocent young men of HAFS, we strongly urge the New Orleans Police Department to search for evidence against the fae who continue to prey on human life. We can no longer turn a blind eye to those who tried to send our world into the blackness of eternal night. Fae creatures with evil magic live among us, and those in HAFS will stand for it no longer."

"He sounds like a lunatic, doesn't he?" Sophie returned to bring Gulliver his check, nodding at the paper clutched in his hands.

"Yeah. The whole thing is kind of unbelievable." Gulliver wasn't sure what to say. That a human newspaper would even mention fae was cause for alarm. Gulliver needed to speak to his father about what they should do next. Fae were being targeted—likely by this HAFS group—and it was up to those of the five kingdoms to bring an end to such suffering. If that meant they could no longer visit the human realm, then that was a price they would have to pay. It was time for the fae living among the humans to come home. It was much too dangerous here.

"Mind if I take this?" Gulliver asked, holding the newspaper up in question.

"Go for it. Customers leave their papers here all the time. There'll be ten more laying around by this afternoon."

"Thanks." Gulliver stood, eager to get back to Toby with this news.

"See you next time," Sophie said in an absent voice.

"Hey, Sophie." Gulliver reached for her hand to stop her. "Take care of yourself." He glanced down at the bruises on her finger. They looked painful and swollen, like someone had touched her in anger. "No one should ever leave marks on you. For any reason." He started to walk away. "Whether you bruise easily or not," he added with a gentle smile. "You are far too kind to deserve that."

He thought he saw her eyes shine with tears before she dropped her head.

"Thanks for the superior snacks," he called over his shoulder as he walked out of the cafe and headed back toward the Lamothe House at a brisk pace.

"Hey, Tobes, you're not going to believe this!" Gulliver burst into their hotel room, expecting to find Toby still in bed or well on his way to getting drunk in the middle of the day. Instead, he found his roommate showered and wearing clean clothes, sitting on the small sofa with Xavier. "Oh, sorry. I didn't realize we had a guest."

"It's just Xavier." Toby shrugged, sipping a cup of hot tea. Gulliver hadn't seen him drink anything other than wine since they arrived, so this was an improvement.

"Have you seen this in the human news?" Gulliver tossed the paper onto the coffee table and sat down on the edge of his bed. "I've seen that man. He was giving Sophie a hard time the other day."

"How do you know Sophie?" Xavier asked. "I wanted to ask the..." He paused, seeming to remember how he'd treated them. "I just couldn't around other people. Sophie, she's..."

"She's a waitress he has a crush on." Toby yawned, looking very uninterested in the conversation. "You'd have known that if you didn't kick us out of your safety house just for mentioning her name."

"I go there for the pastries," Gulliver insisted.

"The beignets at Cafe du Monde are a thousand times better," Toby said.

"Since when do you go out for snacks?"

"Since Xavier made me." They were friends now? Something about that didn't make sense.

Gulliver tried to ignore the warning bells going off in his head, tried to forget this man kicked him and Toby out of their house of safety after the bombing. "Well, I like the ones at Sophie's place, and you would too if you had them fresh."

"Listen to him. Sophie's place," Toby mocked.

"I can't pronounce the Vew Kar-y Caffy."

"It's the Vieux Carré Cafe," Xavier said. "Okay, so you know Sophie. Which means you need to tell me anything she's said about Gabe Christoph?"

"Just that he's a bully, and I'm pretty sure he's the one that kidnapped Sophie in the alley last week. And he's probably the one responsible for her bruises today."

Xavier pulled his feet off the coffee table and placed them on the floor before he leaned toward Gulliver. "Bruises?" he growled. "Are you sure they're from Gabe?"

"Um. I don't know. Honestly, I don't really know anything about her other than that she's nice." A small smile played on his face. "She's really nice to me."

"Her father is dangerous," Xavier said, but there was something off in his words, something he wasn't telling them. "And Gabe is his right-hand man. He's the one responsible for that explosion. The fae communities live in fear of the HAFS groups across the country. But we have ways of hiding and tracking HAFS activities. It could have been a lot worse than it was. The humans don't know how to identify us, so they end up killing their own. Still, we lost six fae in that attack. It has to stop." Xavier sat with his hands clenched in fists as he stared at the image of Gabe in the newspaper.

"Did you say communities? As in more than one?" Gulliver asked. "Across the country?"

"Many more," Xavier said. "Across the world. Most of us fae have been here for generations."

"How?" Gulliver thought they were here to save one small group of fae. He wasn't sure he could handle more than that.

"You two really aren't from around here, are you?"

"Isn't it obvious?" Toby spoke for the first time, still sipping his tea. "We're from the fae home world. I thought I told you I was Prince of Iskalt."

"And I thought you were just drunk and in need of

sobering up." Xavier shrugged. "It doesn't really matter where any of us are from. We're here. This is our world too, and we aren't leaving."

"Even if you could go back to the fae realm, where you could live in peace?" Gulliver leaned forward, his elbows propped on his knees. "I can't imagine how much easier that would be for everyone."

"This is our home. It's all we know, and we aren't leaving."

Chapter Thirteen
SOPHIE-ANN

She shouldn't be here. At work. Out in the world. In fact, all Sophie wanted was to curl up in bed and pretend she was a kid with all her hope for the future still intact.

A coughing fit overtook her, sending a shock of pain through her chest and making it hard to breathe. She bent over, trying to catch her breath. The symptoms were getting worse, and no amount of treatment had helped her much in the last year. The breathing treatments never lasted. The chemo had only made her want to die more quickly.

"Go in the kitchen if you insist on looking so sick." Vicky put a hand on her back, urging her through the swinging door. "Why'd you come in today if you can barely stand?"

Sophie gripped the edge of the metal counter for support. The noisy kitchen was a welcome distraction, but the cooks ignored the intruders. "I need the money."

That was a lie. She'd never needed the income from this

job and she hated waiting tables. But what this job truly provided her was an escape. Even if she'd love to wrap up in a heated blanket in bed, that was too close to her father, to the men and women constantly stopping by.

She could barely look at any of them after the bombing, after their cold disregard for life. And the surprise engagement.

Lucky for her, she'd never have to see the marriage through. Not unless her father forced the matter soon. The announcement was nothing more than politics. Gabe setting himself up as the successor to her father's role in HAFS, and her father desperate to believe she'd still be here when it all came to pass.

He had a toxic optimism, but she was a realist.

Another cough wracked her body. Vicky scowled and walked back into the dining room, leaving Sophie to try to remain standing by herself. Her legs wobbled beneath her, but the weakness was nothing new for her. Both her mind and body lacked the strength this world demanded of her.

"I have to get some air." No one was listening to her, so she edged toward the door to the alleyway, her hands skimming along countertops and walls for support.

When she finally pushed out into the fresh air, she drew a cleansing breath into her burning lungs. Her throat was raw from days of coughing. She was tired of it all. For the last two years, she'd fought. And fought.

There was nothing left in her.

Sliding down the wall, she sat next to the overstuffed trash cans. They didn't smell particularly pleasant, but she couldn't have moved right then if she tried. Pulling her knees in, she rested her forehead against them and closed her eyes, trying to forget where she was, who she was.

Her mother used to tell her she was too good for this world. It was something only someone blinded by love could claim, but she held on to it now, trying to make herself believe that was why she'd be leaving it so soon.

Sweetheart, the good things in this life hide away. You have to go searching for them while the bad try to make you believe you've seen all there is to see.

Her mother's voice was once so clear in her mind, so present. Over the years, it faded until only the words remained. What would her mom think of her now? She may not have set off the bombs, but that didn't mean she was innocent in the recent tragedy.

Most of the world thought HAFS was insane for believing in the fae. To them, the group performed terrorist acts. Now, Gabe was a watched man.

"Fancy seeing you in an alley that smells no better than Bourbon Street." The familiar voice had her lifting her eyes to the man leaning against the wall opposite her.

"Xavier." His name came out on a sob. "What are you doing here?"

"I could ask you the same question?" He pushed off the wall to approach her.

She lifted a shoulder in utter patheticness. "I..." She sighed. "I can't get up."

His face softened. Xavier was one of the only people in the world, other than doctors and family, who knew of her condition. It wasn't by choice. She'd called him after one of her treatments when she could hardly stand. He wouldn't rest until she'd told him everything.

He sat beside her, not saying a word.

Leaning her head on his shoulder, she drew in a deep breath. "Do you ever think about what kind of people we'd be if we'd grown up in a different city? If our parents were still around?"

Both of Xavier's parents were gone. He only had a brother he never mentioned, who he hated, and a grandmother.

He didn't answer her question. "Sometimes, I wonder what this city would be like if we didn't live here. Maybe there'd be peace."

She heard what he wasn't saying. If her father didn't lead HAFS in their attacks, New Orleans might not be the dangerous city it had become. Leaning away from him, she tried to push to her feet. He jumped up to steady her, but she shook her head.

"Why are you here, Xavier? It's been a year." He'd once been her only friend, but over the years, distance grew between them, and it was his doing, his choice. He'd wanted her to fight against HAFS from the inside, but she'd been scared. Terrified, really. Her father was all she had left.

Doing nothing is almost worse than doing wrong, he'd said back then.

Xavier clasped his hands behind his back. "The bombing—"

"No." She couldn't talk about this with him. "I didn't even know it was happening. They abducted me from work and kept me locked up until it was over."

"It was bad, Soph."

"You were there?" Why was she asking? She already knew the answer. Xavier had made a habit of tracking HAFS movements and trying to save as many people as he could. He didn't care if he saved fae along with the humans.

"If you'd seen it, you'd know this war your father is waging needs to be stopped."

"It can't. He can't." She hugged her arms across her chest. "And soon ..." She couldn't voice her biggest fear. When she died, would her father lose it? Would he seek healing through violence?

"Evil can always be stopped."

"He's not ..." Evil? Maybe he was, and she just didn't want to think it.

"I need to know what's next. If there's another target already."

She shook her head. "You don't understand. I'm the gem of HAFS, a stone to be protected, shown off. That's it. They don't involve me in their plans. I didn't hear about the bombing in the French Quarter until after it happened."

He pushed a hand through his hair, clear agitation on his face. "I don't know what to do next. How to stop this from happening."

"Maybe you can't."

His shoulders drooped like the weight of all the future lives he'd lose pulled them toward the ground. Would she have to bury Xavier before she died?

"You should go." She straightened, slivers of her strength returning. "Before someone sees you." She was forbidden from associating with Xavier, and she didn't know what her father or his bulldogs would do if they caught them together.

He didn't move. "There's something else." His lips tugged down. "Gabe ..."

"I didn't have a choice." Tears sprang to her eyes.

"You're engaged to my brother."

All she could do was nod, letting tears flow freely down her cheeks. Gabe and Xavier hated each other for reasons they'd never told her. She was the only person who knew about their relation. They shared a mother but had different fathers and personalities like day and night.

Xavier was so sure, so steady. He wasn't necessarily a happy, smiley man, but there was a gentleness to him that was completely absent in his older brother.

"I tried to say no. My father won't hear it. It's okay," she whispered, forcing a smile. "We all know I'll never have to go through with it."

Xavier pulled her against his chest, wrapping strong arms around her. "Do you need help? I have people ... We can get you out. You'll be safe with us."

She pressed her face into his shirt. He always smelled good, familiar. A mixture of honey and pine. Ignoring his words, she sighed. "A year is too long to go without seeing you."

That was her answer, and she knew he'd understand. She couldn't leave her father, even if what he was doing was so wrong. The mission of the group—pushing fae from their world—was righteous. She didn't agree with their violent methods, but the simple truth was that fae creatures did not belong in this world.

The back door opened, and Sophie expected Vicky to come out and make her get back to work, but a large frame filled the doorway.

"Hello, brother." Gabe grinned, stepping into the alley. "I'd appreciate it if you took your hands off my fiancée."

Sophie didn't want to leave the safety of Xavier, but she pushed him away and wiped the tears from her face.

"You shouldn't be here, Gabe." She attempted a look of concern. "Your face is all over the news."

He scowled. "I couldn't hide out in your father's garden shed any longer. Come here." He gripped her arm, fingertips pressing into the bruises, and yanked her against him.

Peppermint breath hit her moments before his lips touched hers, rough and vindictive. A show for his brother.

Sophie let him kiss her, her body frozen in place.

When he finally yanked himself away, he smiled at Xavier. "I just came for that. Now that we're engaged, I expect a lot more." He slapped her butt, making her jump and yelp in surprise.

Sophie wiped her mouth in disgust, too angry to use her words.

Xavier's eyes narrowed in fury. "If you so much as hurt one hair on her head, I will come for you. Brother or not, I will kill you."

"I prefer the not part of that."

A commotion sounded at the end of the alley as a group of tourists walked by. Gabe pressed himself up against the building.

"You have to go." Sophie shoved him. "And don't you ever touch me like that again."

"This will blow over when your father gives them another fall guy."

She pushed him again. "That day is not today."

Gabe looked from Xavier to Sophie and back before a growl ripped from his throat and he yanked open the door, disappearing inside.

"I should get back to work." She brushed dirt off her butt and the front of her apron.

Xavier's gaze connected with hers. "If you ever decide you want to live the rest of your limited time outside a murderous cult, you know how to reach me. I will do anything to help you, Sophie-Ann. You just have to let me."

"Noted." Her shoulders slumped, and she wondered if anyone would ever get how tired she was of it all. Too tired to fight back.

"And seriously, don't marry that guy, Soph. You're way too good for him." He gave her one last look before heading down the alley toward the main road.

Sophie pushed out a breath, his words running back in her mind. Limited time. She could feel the clock ticking inside her, a time bomb just waiting to hit zero.

And it was closer than anyone else realized.

When she went back to work, she attempted a smile, but it felt as fragile as every other part of her. She reached the dining room and slid into a chair at an empty table, leaning her head on the solid wood. It was all she could do with the meager energy she had left.

"Go home." Vicky sighed. "Come back tomorrow or not at all."

One day soon, it would be not at all.

Chapter Fourteen
GULLIVER

"What do you mean you can't tell me where we're going?" Gulliver stopped Toby on the shaded sidewalk of Esplanade Avenue near their hotel. "I'm not just going to trust Xavier. I've only met him a few times. What do we even know about him?"

Toby stiffened. "It's been more than a few times." He'd grown distant over the last days but differently than before. He wasn't drinking or mooning over Logan. It was like he had too much on his mind.

"That's where you've been?" While Gulliver was at the library combing through articles on bombings and murders, connecting various ones to HAFS so he could send Tia a full report whenever his dad or Loch showed up to check on them, Toby was off making friends. "Tobes, he threw us out of his house."

Gulliver wouldn't forgive that. The mere mention of Sophie got them tossed onto the street by their own kind.

And he wanted to know why. Now, sitting in the room at the inn was a folder detailing every piece of information he could find on Claude Devereaux. Next, Gulliver needed to tackle the internet, but that was a scary place, and he didn't know where to start.

"He had his reasons, I'm sure." Toby turned to Gulliver with a sigh. "He says he can take us to one of the local fae communities."

Gulliver drew up straight. "How many are there just in this city?"

"I don't know. He's slow with the information, but this particular group wants to meet us."

If Tia were here, she'd jump at this chance. Maybe this community would have more information on HAFS. "Fine."

Toby grinned. "Thought you'd see it my way."

They turned onto Bourbon Street, where a white car waited at the curb with a yellow stripe and the word Taxi on it.

"I thought Taxis were supposed to be all yellow," Gulliver whispered, remembering the poor woman they'd abducted at the bus station.

Xavier opened the passenger door. "Get in."

A pale woman with wild black curls sat behind the steering thing. She had a metal ring piercing her lip and a bar in her eyebrow.

"Good day." Gulliver leaned forward to offer her his hand. "I'm Lord Gulliver O'Shea."

She and Xavier shared a look, both hiding their smiles.

"Lane." She shook her head. "And there ain't no fae lords in this world, Your Highness."

"Oh, I'm not a prince." Gulliver's face reddened. "But Toby here is."

Toby elbowed him. "Will you shut up?"

Lane hit the gas, and they sped forward at a too-fast clip. She narrowly missed hitting a woman in a bright outfit covered in some kind of shiny material. Gulliver didn't stop gripping the edge of the seat until they were out of the city.

The roads were crowded with cars, and the landscape was marred by giant metal structures. He wondered if the cities of the human realm had ever held the beauty of Fargelsi or Iskalt.

Music blared from the box built into the car. Gulliver had never been particularly fond of human music, and this made his ears hurt with its screeching voice and a thumping he felt all the way to his bones.

Toby didn't seem to mind as his head bobbed to the beat.

"Where are we going?" Gulliver yelled over the awful sound.

Xavier looked back, studying him. "A place called Chalmette. Our communities keep a low profile, sticking mostly to the nondescript suburbs where we can blend in."

Gulliver didn't know what a suburb was, but if that's where the fae lived, it must be a beautiful place. They passed old houses with boards in place of windows. Walls leaned in like they'd cave at any moment, and some had missing chunks of their roofs.

Any moment now, they'd get to the wide-open spaces fae loved. The rolling hills and greenery. There'd be horizons as fine as paintings and fresh fruit ripe on the trees.

But that never came. Instead, they drove through neighborhoods of squashed together homes, cracked roads, and so many of those shops humans loved.

Disappointment hit him when they pulled up to a small house with peeling brown paint, a sinking porch, and a faded red door.

"This is ... it?" Gulliver tried to get Toby to meet his gaze, but his eyes were firmly fixed on Xavier.

"It's where we meet." Xavier stepped out of the car.

"Meet for what?" Something about this didn't feel right, but Gulliver couldn't quite put his tail on it.

"Stop with the questions, Gullie." Toby frowned. "I'm sure we'll find out."

Gulliver had never known Toby to lack curiosity or common caution. He was Tia O'Shea's twin, after all. Sure, she never backed down and barged into places she shouldn't, but she also recognized when something was wrong.

Xavier seemed trustworthy, but Gulliver didn't trust anyone who wasn't part of his family. He'd learned that the hard way. From growing up in the prison realm to suffering in the Vondurian dungeons, his experiences taught him even the right reasons could cause evil.

"Why'd we take a cab here?" Gulliver wouldn't stop asking questions. It wasn't in him.

"Because cabs go mostly unnoticed." Lane stepped through the door. "We're back!"

Heads popped out of doorways, fae appearing like those white-faced people with colorful hair Tia once made him watch pile out of a small car.

"You brought friends." A broad man lumbered forward, wings sprawling out behind him. At his side was a small older woman, her eyes flashing pale green. Was she using magic, or was that a trick of his imagination?

The door slammed behind them, and Gulliver did his best not to jump. Magic didn't scare him, not anymore. He didn't grow up around it, but since the prison magic broke, he'd spent more time than he'd admit with the most powerful magic wielder of all the fae.

Xavier dropped a bag on a beat-up settee with a tear across one cushion. Shiny gray stuff covered it. "This is Gulliver and Toby. They're from ... there." That's all he said to describe the vast world beyond this one, but the fae crowding the living room nodded as if they understood. "They came to investigate what's happening with HAFS."

"And what have you learned?" The big man crossed his arms.

Gulliver rubbed the back of his neck. "They're killing fae and any humans accused of being fae."

Silence. And then, laughter wound through the group.

"Astute observation." Lane lifted one brow. "Tell me, how did you come by such top secret information?"

"All right." Xavier held up a hand. "Leave them alone. They're trying to help." He looked at Gulliver and Toby. "You are, right?"

Both men nodded.

"Perfect. Well, you're just in time." He sat on the back of the settee.

"Time for what?" Gulliver looked from gleeful face to gleeful face.

"We've watched our fae die for too long. Our human allies have sacrificed their lives. We can't keep sitting still and doing nothing. We have to fight back."

A cheer wound through the room, fae high fiving and smiling.

Despite the muggy air, a chill settled into Gulliver.

Toby grinned along with the rest. "What are we planning?"

We. That didn't take long.

Lane clapped him on the shoulder. "Just know, if you betray us, we will kill you, fae or not."

"I'd never betray the fae." Toby clenched his fists. "The humans have to be held to account."

There it was. His reason. He needed to take his revenge on anyone he could blame for fae pain. Logan died at the hands of the fire plains. There was no vindication to be had there. But here there was an enemy he could fight.

Xavier jumped off the back of the couch and walked toward a smaller room, where a table sat with maps spread out before it. "We've chosen our targets. We have our supplies." He pressed the map flat as it started to curl up. "Here." He pointed to something directly in the center of the city. "We can get word to the nearby fae communities and our human allies to avoid this area. Then, we take out an entire block."

Many sets of eyes flashed different colors, and Gulliver knew exactly what they were thinking. That this would show them. The fae had been pushed too far.

"What about the other humans?" Gulliver asked. "The ones who know nothing of fae and don't believe in the mission of HAFS?"

Lane shrugged. "We can't let collateral damage hold us back. The only way to preserve our fae is to fight."

This wasn't okay. Gulliver shook his head, backing up. "I

have been to war. Twice. I've seen the true damage it can do when unleashed."

They all stared at him like he was some kind of creature who didn't belong. He guessed he was. "I've been to war too." Toby's voice was soft. "I've lost people I love. But it's taught me that short-term violence is sometimes necessary for long-term peace."

"You can't believe that." The only time war was justifiable was to fight back against evil. This would only antagonize it, embolden it. It wasn't a fight. It was suicide.

"So, the two sides are just going to keep killing those who have nothing to do with this waiting for the other to give in?" Gulliver's back hit the wall. "This isn't what our queen sent us here for, Toby."

"My sister wants HAFS dealt with."

"We're gathering information. That's our role."

"She sent me with you to get me out of her hair. You can continue your mission, but I will choose one for myself."

Gulliver turned and ducked through the doorway, not looking back as he headed across the house. He could hardly breathe until he reached the front stoop.

A raindrop hit his cheek, and he peered up into an angry sky. With no way to get home, all he could do was wait. Wait for Toby to come to his senses, for the fae here to realize attacking humans was not the way to gain their freedom. Too many people were going to die.

He sat on the stone step and buried his face in his hands. His tail curled around him, as if trying to comfort him. He'd learned long ago he couldn't stop those bent on destruction.

"Tia," Gulliver whispered, "I wish you were here." He'd thought he and Toby were in this together, that they'd do their duty and then report to the queen so she could decide what actions needed to be taken. But he was wrong.

Gulliver was very much alone.

The door opened behind him, and he didn't lift his head when Xavier took a seat at his side. Neither spoke at first, and the rain came down harder. The small overhang protected them to an extent, but Gulliver could still feel spritzes of water dampening his clothes.

"You don't want to be here, do you?" Xavier peered into the rain, looking for answers.

It took Gulliver a moment to answer. "My queen sent me."

"That doesn't answer my question."

"Someone needed to come. Why not me?" Gulliver had asked himself that question his entire life. As a child, when he entered Lord Kvek's fortress to steal food. Why shouldn't it be Gulliver keeping his village fed? In the war of the four kingdoms, he was a ten-year-old who did impossible things, and why shouldn't he? When Tia wanted to save the kingdom that held her prisoner as the fire plains expanded, he'd stood at her side. There was no reason not to.

He was Gulliver, an orphan turned son of a prince, best friend of a queen. A dark fae with no offensive magic. It didn't take someone who was born "special," someone with an obvious fate, to do the right thing.

Xavier rubbed his chin. "I don't understand you."

"Few fae do." Only Tia. She would know what he was trying to say without him having to explain it. One must always fight for good, fight to protect as many lives as possible. It was the harder choice, the unpopular one, but to fae like him or Tia and her parents, it was the only choice there was.

"Sophie." Xavier breathed out her name like it was sacred to him.

Gulliver's gaze snapped to his. "You mean the woman whose very name made you and your friends throw me out onto the street?"

Xavier closed his eyes for a fraction of a second, and when he opened them, there was a softness that hadn't existed as he'd instructed his fae on how to make war with the unsuspecting humans. "Let's just say I've known her for a long time, and I have very personal reasons for wanting to destroy HAFS. You want another way? I'm giving you one."

"What are you talking about?"

"She is the key. Her father leads the New Orleans sector of HAFS, and if circumstances were different, she'd be the obvious successor."

No. Gulliver couldn't think, couldn't feel. The waitress who entranced him the moment he saw her, the one with bright smiles and sad eyes ... she was part of this? Part of the group who hated his kind?

"We watch her, watch who she talks to. You've been at the diner nearly every day since your arrival. There's no use denying the connection between you two. This war is coming to New Orleans. We are fighting back. The only way to stop us is to destroy HAFS. From the inside."

Gulliver jerked back, his cat eyes widening and his tail going completely still. "You want me to get closer to her."

He nodded reluctantly.

"Become one of them."

Again, a nod was the only answer.

"And what then?"

"We help you kill Claude Devereaux and his lieutenants."

Kill? Sophie's father? "Will that prevent fae attacks?"

Xavier's brows drew together. "The humans must pay for what they've done, but it will bring a swifter end to this war if we can cut off one of their leaders."

Gulliver stood, looking down at Xavier. This man wanted him to become an assassin surrounded by those who hated him, an island in an angry storm. And doing so wouldn't even prevent the deaths from coming. "That's not my mission. I am loyal to my queen."

He started off down the driveway.

"Think about it, Gullie," Xavier called after him.

He wouldn't. His answer was the one his conscience could handle. Yet, there was so much to what Xavier said that his heart couldn't.

Sophie was one of them. HAFS. The humans wanted to survive, but didn't they see so many more of them would die because of their hatred?

Good, sweet Sophie. Was the abduction from her diner a ruse?

An ache rested inside his chest as he walked down the road. Cars passed, some pulling into a lane next to a strange building that sold something called a daiquiri from a window. There was an acrid, dense smell to the air that couldn't be erased by the rain falling from the heavy clouds above. Water dripped into his eyes, and he didn't bother wiping it away.

How far was it back to the city? All he wanted was to go home to the green fields of Myrkur or the icy shores of Iskalt, where the air froze a fae's eyelashes to their cheeks while also cleansing them with the scent of the sea.

A car pulled up to the curb in front of him. "Need a ride?" the driver called.

"A taxi," Gulliver whispered. A real one this time. It said it right on the side, but then so had Xavier and Lane's car. Walking to the city wasn't an option, so he threw himself into the backseat.

A blast of cold air hit him, and he hugged his arms across his chest for warmth.

"Oh, sorry, kid," the man said. "Had the AC on full blast, but you must be freezing your knickers off."

"I'm not sure what knickers are, sir, but I'm sure I still have them. Just a little wet."

He let out a bellowing laugh.

"Is this a real taxi? I don't want to make you drive anywhere you do not wish to. Please know I do not plan to abduct you."

The man pulled onto the road, chuckling to himself. "Good to know. Didn't you read the side? Taxi. That's me. I'll take you to the moon if you can pay."

Gulliver pulled the damp plastic card from his pocket. "Does this still work when it's wet?"

"You're a hoot. Yes, it'll work. Just remember you want to give Jerry here a fat tip. Where am I taking you?"

Gulliver gave the name of Sophie's cafe without a second thought. He had to see her, had to look into her eyes and search for the hate that must reside there.

The old man up front prattled on about traffic, yelling at other cars and raising a finger at them. It was all very strange. By the time they reached the Vieux Carré Cafe, Gulliver almost needed to throw up. He pushed the card through the machine and hit the button for tips, selecting the biggest one. With a quick thank you, he stepped out.

The taxi sped off, leaving Gulliver alone on the sidewalk. He peered into the wide windows, looking for her. There were no patrons around the tables, and he assumed the rain scared them off.

And then, she was there. Sophie breezed out of the kitchen like a Fargelsian summer, light and airy. She worked to clear tables, a slowness to her movements. He suspected she was in no hurry without any customers to serve. A small smile tilted the corners of her mouth, and her lips moved. It took a moment for Gullie to realize she was singing to herself.

How could this woman be a member of a group bent on killing and destruction? He'd known a lot of evil people, and one thing he'd learned was that there were clues. Long before they ever did wrong, their behaviors predicted the future.

But not her. In his weeks coming here, Gulliver sensed two strong things in her. Kindness and a strange sadness. Not ill intent, not even a mean word spoken.

The bell over the door made a soft jingling sound as he entered, and she looked up from where she stacked dishes on her tray, her smile finally reaching her eyes. "Gulliver."

"Hi." He wasn't sure what else to say, how to talk to a woman who hated everything he represented.

"If you have a seat, I'll be right with you." She walked toward the kitchen with her tray. There was something even more fragile to her than normal today. Each step looked like a conscious move instead of the habit of walking humans and fae alike developed.

Could Gulliver do it? Could he get close to this woman simply to reach her father? Even if Tia gave him that exact order, he wasn't sure. Lying to her felt like lying to himself, to his soul.

Sophie returned, pulling paper and a pen from her apron. "Just beignets today? Or are you here for dinner? The rain kind of kept the dinner rush away, so I'm hoping you'll be here a while."

Gulliver's face flushed with warmth. "I'll be here as long as you want me to be." Until he went back to the world she'd destroy if she had the chance.

Her eyes met his, and he did it. He searched for any clues he'd missed, any way he'd misread her. There was nothing. Only a softness he'd grown to appreciate. Also, a hidden strength, the kind that only came about after extreme trials. He recognized it because Tia wore the same look in her eyes. Like every day they woke up, it was in defiance of the very world.

"So," she coughed, her breath wheezing in her chest. "Dinner?"

"You don't look so well." He stood, reaching for her arm to guide her into a chair.

"I'm fine. It's just been a long day." Her eyes clouded over, a film keeping her secrets inside.

Her entire body slumped in the chair, and she whispered, "I'm okay," before falling sideways onto the cold tile floor.

Chapter Fifteen
SOPHIE-ANN

Am I dead?

That was the first thought rolling through Sophie's mind before she opened her eyes. Maybe she dreaded it, or maybe she hoped it was true this time, but whatever her circumstances were, she'd learned long ago that she had to accept them.

Dying wasn't easy for anyone, let alone someone who should have their entire life ahead of them. She used to sit high up in her room, watching people out her double-paned window. They laughed and smiled, making plans for their futures.

She'd spent so long forced only to live in the present. But had she truly been alive?

"Sophie," a soft voice called to her. For a moment, she thought it was her mother welcoming her home. A hand gripped hers, and she smiled.

"I think she's waking up." This voice held less care, less

regard for her. She didn't need to see the speaker to know that. "You can leave now."

"Not a chance."

They were still arguing when her eyelids fluttered open, so they didn't see her stir. Two men stood above her bed, both tall. One was broader, but the other was a sea of calm in the middle of her storm.

She wasn't with her mom, didn't get to see her quite yet, but Gulliver quelled the panic inside. It wasn't over, as much as she wished it were. Being dead would be an upgrade over dying, and yet, she wanted to hear his voice again.

"Gullie," she whispered, unable to get more volume into her voice.

Gabe pushed Gulliver out of the way. "Sophie-Ann, you scared us." She knew what really scared him. That she'd die before he could formally entrench himself in her family as Claude's prized son-in-law. He touched her arm, and she flinched away.

"Where's my dad?" she managed. Whatever he'd done, whoever he was, the one thing she knew was he'd be by her side until the end.

Gulliver opened his mouth to speak, but Gabe cut him off.

"The hospital called your house, but he wasn't there. One of the guys answered and got a message to me."

It was her house, but it really belonged to them. The people of HAFS. They came and went at all hours, and she couldn't even die in the presence of only her father because others would hear about it.

Gulliver rounded the bed to the opposite side of Gabe.

He didn't touch her, something she was grateful for. "He's coming."

She nodded, trying to swallow. Her tongue stuck to the roof of her mouth. It was so dry. More than anything, she just wanted water and peace, but neither seemed possible at the moment. An IV in her arm kept her from reaching too far, and the drugs they pumped into her turned her brain to mush.

At this point in her illness, nurses and doctors no longer pretended there were treatment options to look into. Every time she ended up in the hospital, all they could do was load her up with pain medications and wait to see if that was it for her.

It never was. At least, not yet. One day soon, she'd finally get her painless sleep.

Her head pounded, and she squinted against the bright white fluorescents they seemed determined to torture patients with in every hospital she'd seen. "Gabe." She turned her gaze on him, making her voice quiver on the way out. "Can you find him? Please."

Gabe took her hand in his. "I will. And then, you and I need to talk. I love you, Soph. I don't want to wait to marry you because then I may never get the chance. All those times I called you lazy ... I didn't know. I swear."

She'd have said anything to get him out of the room. "Tomorrow." She wouldn't have to go through with it if she died before then.

Gabe leaned down, pressing a kiss to her lips, and she did her best not to gag. When he left, shutting the door behind him, her shoulders relaxed and she released a breath.

Gulliver was silent for a long moment. "You're going to marry him?"

"No." She tried to lift her head, but she didn't have the strength. "I don't know if it'll get that far."

The heavy meaning of her words sat between them, the silence stifling. She didn't really know if today was the day she never went home again. Episodes like this over the last few months weren't rare, but they'd gotten exponentially worse each time. Her doctors forbid her from working, from taxing herself, but the alternative was to die an unremarkable death in the house that sometimes felt more like a prison.

She'd wanted to be out in the world, to see people and remind herself life would go on without her. It was a strange sort of comfort. Not even Vicky knew how sick she was. There were other terms she'd used to describe her.

Clumsy. Lazy. Incompetent.

From her constant need to sit down to the frequent falls, it was all true. And yet, it wasn't her truth.

Gulliver crossed the room and pulled a heavy recliner toward the bed. It scraped against the tile floor. Once he'd positioned it, he reached for the tray near her bed, picking up the giant cup. It had a lid and a straw, but there was no way she had the strength to hold it.

He didn't ask her to. Instead, he positioned the straw against her lips. She tried to draw water into it, but when none came, tears welled in her eyes. She was helpless, and that was a feeling she'd sought to avoid at all costs.

Sensing her distress, Gulliver took off the lid and tilted the cup against her lips, letting a tiny trickle enter her parched mouth. More, she needed more.

"Careful," he cautioned, setting the cup back down. "You should only have a little at a time."

"Why ..." She drew in a breath, trying to gather the strength to speak. "You're here."

He sat in the recliner, crossing one leg over the other. A soft smile tilted his lips when he looked at her. She'd never gotten the chance to study him this closely before, to look into his clear eyes and find out what was behind the mystery that seemed to follow him.

Now, they were here, and all she could do was stare at him. At the way his smile was slightly crooked, his irises larger than normal. They were like a window into his soul. The look he gave her infused warmth into her chilled limbs.

"I'm the one who brought you here. I got one of those helper cars."

"A taxi?"

He nodded. "Do you remember what happened?"

She nodded. The restaurant. Falling. Darkness. "But you stayed."

"You needed me to." He shrugged like it wasn't a big deal, but to her, it was. Other than her parents, she'd never had anyone do anything for her without wanting something in return. Even Gabe ... He wanted to marry her to become her father's successor, the son he never had. And when she was gone, he'd be the only child of Claude Devereaux left. No one would care if it was by blood or marriage.

"Thank you." She attempted a smile, but her face felt numb, like it was frozen in place.

Gulliver leaned forward, elbows on his knees. "I still don't understand what happened. The healer who stopped by seemed to know you, but she wouldn't tell me anything."

There was anxiety in his voice, a true worry. Sophie barely knew this man as anything more than her favorite customer, but something inside of her screamed to trust him.

That maybe he was the only one she *could* trust.

"I'm sick."

"I see that." Gulliver's brow furrowed. "But places like this give you herbs, right? And tonics that can make you better?"

Her eyelids were heavy, but she struggled to keep them open. "Not for me. No medicine can cure cancer once it's spread into as many organs as it has in me."

"Cancer." Confusion clouded his face, as if he'd never heard the word. "Like a plague?"

"You're right. It is a plague. One I won't survive."

His eyes glassed over, and she wished she could take her words back, that she could return his smile with one of her own. "No. You're young. Even humans don't die this young. It's a lie."

In her drug-addled mind, a warning signal told her there was something off in his words, but she didn't have the energy to consider them more closely. "No lies." She sighed, and it felt like her entire chest caved in, squeezing her lungs. The heart monitor to her left started beeping, a familiar rhythm to her life.

Darkness enveloped her before she blinked her tired eyes open again. Doctors rushed into the room, yelling at Gulliver to get out of the way. She vaguely remembered the panic on his face, the redness in his eyes.

Don't cry for me, she wanted to say. *I'll be okay*.

Her throat seized up, and her entire body jerked as pain seared into her chest.

"Again," a doctor shouted.

"Charge to two hundred." One of the nurses pressed the cool paddles against her chest once again. "Clear!"

This time, when the world faded away, she sank into the darkness, welcoming its cold embrace.

Still not dead.

Wasn't that a shame?

Her father refused to let her sign a DNR, to let her die in peace. And every single person in this hospital knew enough to fear him.

"You saved my daughter," she heard him say. "Young man, I don't know you, but if there's anything you need in this city, all you have to do is ask."

"Thank you, sir." Gulliver's voice was soft yet strong. "But I really just want to stay to make sure she's okay."

"She is. Thanks to you."

Sophie forced her eyes open. Every part of her hurt, and she wondered how many more times she'd have to wake like this. Feeling a familiar button in her hand, she hit it twice, waiting for the morphine to take over.

"Honey." Her dad stood when he saw her awake and rushed to the bed. "We've been so worried."

Tears crusted in the corners of her eyes, and if she had more in her, they'd probably stream down her face. Instead, all she had was a barely audible, scratchy voice. "Why can't you let me go?"

His mask fell, and she realized how exhausted he looked.

His suit, normally pressed to within an inch of its life, sat wrinkled on his frame. Even his hair refused to behave. The last time she'd seen him so destroyed was after her mother died. "You're my baby girl."

"I know." She flipped her hand over, palm up. It was all the movement she could make. He slid his hand into hers. "I can't keep doing this."

"But you were fine. Working, coming to HAFS meetings. Only days ago."

He didn't get it. "I wasn't fine." Those in pain, the sick, hid in plain sight. They didn't let others see how much they struggled, how much they needed. She'd tried for too long not to be the sick girl, the dying girl. Yet, one cannot escape their fate. "Let me go to her, Dad. Please."

She'd never seen the man cry, not even at her mom's funeral. But there were tears in his eyes now. "I can't."

"You mean you won't."

He bent over her hand, his tears warm against her skin. "You're all I have left."

"You'll still have me even after I'm gone." Like she had her mother. Always and forever.

Gulliver cleared his throat, but it wasn't to interrupt. She could tell by the way the man was openly weeping. "I'll ..." sniff, "... give you two some time." Despite the tears, there was a purpose in his eyes she didn't understand, some knowledge that kept him from completely breaking down.

She wondered if she'd ever get to learn what it was.

Chapter Sixteen
GULLIVER

Tia would say this city sucked. It was one of those human phrases she thought was hilarious. She'd complain about the dirty streets that smelled like bodily fluids he didn't want to think about. She wouldn't like the uneven sidewalks, which was odd because sidewalks were a very human creation. Yet, the O'Shea in her would say, if you're going to do something, do it well.

Still, Gulliver had loved it here. The buildings looked like they were straight out of a humantale of the best kind. Bright colors and people from so many places. It was a melding of human cultures he'd found beautiful. That kind of thing didn't happen in the fae realms. Even in Myrkur, where there were fae of all types, one tended to stick to their own.

For someone like Gullie, who had no one else like him, it could be lonely.

But now, this beautiful city had turned sour in his stomach. When he went home, he wouldn't think of all the ways it amazed him. Instead, he'd see a girl, with the most beautiful blue hair, lying in bed, looking as if death called her name. Looking as if she wanted to answer.

Maybe it was despair. She knew this was the end, so she hoped it came quickly. Maybe it was the impending marriage she didn't want, one that couldn't last but would ensure her legacy lived on within a terrorist organization, a group he still couldn't believe she had any part in.

It was raining by the time he reached the inn after wandering the streets for longer than he'd intended. He hadn't seen Toby since the meeting Xavier had taken them to, and he couldn't face him when the only thing he wanted was to take away Sophie's pain.

He stood in the courtyard, contemplating heading back out for another wet stroll, but he couldn't put this off forever. If he could only talk to Tia, he'd let her know what was happening and she'd have the answers. He was sure of it.

But she wasn't here, so it was up to him.

"I am the hero of this story," he whispered to himself as he approached the stairs. He'd never felt like a hero. He was the sidekick, the loyal friend of those who were meant to save the day.

For Sophie, he had to change the story.

There was one conclusion he'd come to since leaving the healers. He could save her, but he wasn't sure she would ever forgive him for what it would take to accomplish such a feat.

When he opened the door to his room, he found Toby and Xavier huddled together near the window. They broke apart when they noticed his presence. Gulliver didn't know what to say, or how to ask Toby for something he wasn't sure he had a right to ask.

"How is she?" Worry etched into every line of Xavier's face. Toby had contacted him after he heard from Gullie. He clearly loved Sophie too, despite the drastic actions he wanted to take against her people.

"Not good." Gulliver stripped off his wet shirt and threw it in a heap in the corner. "I need a hot shower." The air conditioning pushed the damp chill from the rain right into his bones. He needed to gather his strength before entering into the argument with Toby.

Because that was what it would be. A fight. A duel. Their wills pushing against each other until one of them broke.

He kicked off the rest of his clothes on his way to the bathroom. Once the shower heated, he stepped under the hot spray. His tail quivered with pleasure, even as his eyes filled with the tears he thought himself empty of.

"I need guidance, Tia." He rested his forehead against the cold tile wall. The mission was to stay in the human realm to gather intelligence. That was all. Now, Toby was involved in some kind of plot, and Gulliver was considering breaking a sacred rule of the fae. Bringing a human through the portal.

It was more of an unspoken rule than anything else, but there was a reason Myles always had to visit his parents and not the other way around. Other than Myles, the last time a fae brought a human into the fae realm was when Brea was swapped with a human baby. Alona.

"Gullie." Toby's uncertain voice reached him through the pattering of the shower.

"I need a few minutes." He couldn't face him until he scrubbed the desperation from his face. The tears couldn't leave this shower.

"I'm ..." He paused. "I'm sorry about your friend."

For a moment, he sounded like the old Toby. The one who was never far from his sister's side, who was quick to smile but slow to speak. He'd grown up in a magical world and possessed little magic of his own. Like Gulliver, he was different.

Gulliver pushed his anger aside and opened the shower curtain enough to stick his head out. "Thanks for saying that."

Toby shifted from one foot to the other. "Tia never should have sent me with you."

Gulliver reached behind him to shut off the shower and then grabbed a towel. He wrapped it around his waist and stepped out. "Your sister always knows what she's doing." Would even she hate him for what he wanted to do?

"I guess." Toby rubbed the back of his neck.

Hesitating for a moment, Gulliver put a hand on his shoulder and squeezed. He walked past him into their room, where Xavier sat on Toby's bed with a book on his lap.

Xavier looked up and whistled. "Didn't know you were hiding all that behind the tail, Gullie."

He looked down at his chest, not sure what Xavier meant. "Do fae in the human realm have different skin?"

Behind him, Toby laughed. "He's not going to understand you, Xav. Leave him alone."

Xav? Toby already used a nickname for him. Gulliver wasn't sure how he felt about the new closeness between his friend and a fae who knew nothing of their world, one that sought revenge.

As Gulliver dressed, Toby and Xavier spoke in hurried whispers. When he'd had enough of their secrecy, Gulliver turned. "Sophie is going to die."

That stopped both of them.

Xavier hung his head. "She's been sick a long time." He closed his eyes for only a moment. "I wish there was something we could do to help her."

"There is." Gulliver crossed his arms over his chest, his gaze locking with Toby's. "I'm taking her to Lenya."

"No." With that single word, Toby walked from the room. He didn't stop when he reached the pouring rain in the courtyard.

"Seriously, Toby?" Gulliver shouted after him. "You're not even going to talk about it?" He'd just warmed up from his last jaunt in the rain, but that didn't stop him from running to catch up with Toby before he reached the gate to the street.

Grabbing Toby's arm, he forced him to turn.

Toby wouldn't meet his eyes. "You know it's not possible, Gullie."

"You're wrong. Just because something isn't acceptable doesn't mean it's impossible."

"Fine, then I'll just say I won't do it."

"Why not?"

"Oh, I don't know. How about the fact that not a single

royal would sanction such an act? Not even my sister, and we both know she loves wild ideas."

"There's one who would, and you know it." Gulliver released Toby and stepped back.

Toby's jaw clenched. "Then, it's a good thing my mother is no longer in power." Tia may have been a little wild, she may have loved human phrases and food, but only Brea was truly connected to them. Only she was nuts enough to try something like this.

Well, the only royal. Gulliver knew who it was he really needed, but Griff had no power in the courts.

Toby pushed a hand through his sopping wet hair and blew water from his lips. "What do you expect our healers to do for her that hers cannot?"

Thunder crashed overhead, and Xavier yelled from the balcony. "You two idiots ready to come inside yet?"

They both ran toward the winding staircase and didn't stop until they were inside, puddles forming at their feet. Gulliver's chest heaved, and he struggled to catch his breath.

Xavier threw a towel at him, and it smacked him in the face before he caught it. Despite the muggy air outside, he was freezing. Again. He dreamed of crawling into his bed in the small house he'd built near his parents' in Myrkur. Of having his sisters sneak in to curl up against him, their wings wrapping around them in a cocoon.

But he couldn't go back when he knew there was a girl here who deserved to be saved. "I wasn't planning on taking her to a healer."

"Then, what—" Toby's eyes narrowed. "You can't be serious."

"Like a bear attack."

Xavier suppressed a smile. "The phrase is 'like a heart attack'."

Gulliver frowned. "And why is your heart attacking you?" He shook his head. "No, you must be wrong. That doesn't make any sense." Heart attacks? How ridiculous.

Toby growled. "No one cares! What I care about is the fact that Gulliver wants to take Sophie to a place most fae aren't even supposed to know about. It probably wouldn't even work on a human."

"You don't know that."

"What I do know is Eavha and Declan are guarding it for a reason. If others found out what we possessed ..."

Xavier looked from one to the other. "I'm missing something."

Toby turned to him, fire in his eyes. "Xav, I think it's time you went home." He shoved him toward the door. "I'll be at the meeting tomorrow."

"But—" Xavier's protest was cut off by the door slamming in his face.

Toby whirled to face Gulliver again. "You can't take her to the healing pools." Fully restored to its original glory, the healing pools of Lenya were now the most powerful magic in all the fae realms, able to bring back fae from the brink of death. Since allying with Lenya, the council of royals decided not to publicly share knowledge of the pools until they knew how to handle the demand for such unknown magic. Magic with equally unknown consequences.

If they weren't cautious, Lenya would be overrun with those who wanted to control it.

This was all Gulliver had, his only plan. If he could get

Sophie there in time, she might stand a chance. "Please, Toby."

"She's human. They live shorter lives than us for a reason. They hold less value. I am—"

"Less value? Do you even hear yourself right now?" Gulliver gave him a horrified look. This was not the Toby he'd known since they were kids.

"I am sorry for you, Gullie. I really am, but death cannot be defeated." He was thinking of Logan. Gulliver could see it in his eyes.

"What if it can this time?" They wouldn't know if they didn't try.

"It doesn't matter if it can." He sighed. "She's human and therefore not our responsibility."

Gulliver stepped back, the chill no longer from his wet clothes. "How did I not see it before?"

"What are you talking about?"

"You hate them. The humans. You wonder why they get to live while Logan, a fae, had to die. Don't you see? You're just as bad as them, as HAFS. They despise us because we're a threat to them. They don't understand us. That's how you feel about them."

"If you love them so much, Gul, then you should stay here and live where none of them can see the features that make you so much better than them. You'd love that, wouldn't you? To never have to be different again?"

"Careful what you say next." Gulliver's fists clenched at his sides. "I have forgiven a lot, we all have, as you moped around Iskalt. You're treading dangerously close to the point where I give up on you entirely."

Toby stepped closer, dropping his voice. "What do you

think happens when she goes through the portal? When you're no longer just the cute human guy she's been flirting with at the cafe? Do you think she'll rejoice when she sees the tail growing from your backside?"

"I don't know."

"Yes, you do. She hates us simply for who we are. Don't forget who she is and what she has been raised to believe. Make no mistake, Gulliver, that girl is not our ally."

"You don't know her." Gulliver refused to give up on her just because of who her father was. He'd seen something in Sophie, a desire to escape the trap she'd found herself in.

"No, you're right. But I know you. You're different. You will always be different. Everyone in the fae realm sees it, and if you take her there, so will she."

Gulliver lunged, knocking Toby back onto the bed. His fist connected to Toby's cheek, but Toby didn't fight back. "Hit me again, Gullie. I deserve it."

Gulliver froze, staring down into the face of a man who used to be one of his greatest friends, one who wanted to feel pain. Maybe it would be the first thing he felt in many months.

"No." He rolled off him. "If you want to get yourself killed, Toby, you'll have to find someone else to do it."

Toby sat up. "I won't open a portal for you." He pushed to his feet. "Let the human die. You'll get over it." He didn't say another word as he yanked open the door and left Gulliver in the silence of their room.

Toby was reckless, just looking for a fight. Gulliver wanted to go after him, to make sure he didn't do anything stupid, but he didn't because Toby's words echoed in his mind.

You're different. You will always be different.

The words Gulliver feared. The ones that defined his life.

And yet, words that bolstered him now. Yes, he was different, and that meant he wouldn't give up on Sophie, not until she took her last breath.

Chapter Seventeen

SOPHIE-ANN

"Relax, Sophie," the nurse crooned as he stuck her with another syringe full of chemicals. "This will help you feel better."

"I'd rather just go home without the drugs." She winced as the needle left her tender arm. "And let nature take its course." Sophie glanced down at her arm covered in bruises from the treatments her father insisted on.

"Honey." The nurse moved to sit on the edge of the bed, taking Sophie's hand in his. "Your leukemia is at an advanced stage, and your father fought hard to get you into this clinical trial. You and I both know the time you have left is short. This treatment will probably give you a few more weeks. Maybe a month. Your dad wants you to have that time."

"Why prolong the inevitable?" Sophie stared into the young man's eyes. He was the only one who had met her gaze all day. And she hadn't even bothered to learn his name.

"If you want to stop the treatment, you're old enough to speak for yourself."

Sophie turned her head away from the nurse, looking out the window at the hazy clouds in the blue sky. "I can't tell him no." Tears filled her eyes. She'd never been able to tell her father no when it came to what he wanted for her. That was how she'd ended up working at the cafe in the first place. It was how she'd found herself engaged to a man she despised even after she'd said no at first. There was no acknowledgement of her refusal, just the acceptance that she'd do as told eventually.

"Then, you're going to suffer through some horrible weeks ahead if you can't be honest with him. This treatment will buy you more time, and you'll probably have some good days, but the bad days are going to be bad." The nurse brushed the short strands of her blue hair away from her face, and she half wondered if it would all fall out again. She didn't want to be on display at the funeral home with her bald head shining under the lights. She'd never worn a wig before when her hair had fallen out after chemotherapy. She'd made bald work for her. She just didn't want to die like that.

"I can help you talk to him if you want. It's nearly time to talk to you both about hospice care, so you can at least go home."

"Thank you." Sophie squeezed his hand. "I appreciate it, but I've got to be the one to do it." She moved to sit up, trying to get comfortable, but it was just too much work. Sophie wanted to die in her own bed. Not in a hospital surrounded by her father's people who insisted on visiting around the clock.

Even now, several HAFS members lingered in the hall with her father after the nurse had chased them out of her room for her treatment. They'd come flocking back in as soon as he left.

"I can give you something to help you sleep and keep you comfortable." The nurse stood and punched some numbers into his rolling cart, and a drawer popped open with the magic drugs that would send her back to oblivion.

"Thank you." Sophie lay back on the bed, completely exhausted from the treatment that was only going to make her feel worse.

"Hey, champ." Her father peeked into the room with Gabe on his heels. "Up for some company?" He gestured over his shoulder. "Half the leadership is waiting to hear how your treatment went."

"It's just like all the others, Dad," she said, her voice a weak rasp in her throat. "It leaves bruises, burns up my veins, and makes me sicker than I already am."

"But it's going to make you better. You'll see." He sat in the chair beside her bed and took her hand.

"I'm not up for visitors." She glared at Gabe. "I need to talk to my dad. Alone."

"Anything you say to him, you can say to me, Soph. I'm your fiancé."

She wanted to laugh, but it hurt too much. "I seem to recall throwing this ring back in your face." She lifted her hand and clawed the ring off her finger again, tossing it on the table beside her bed. She could just imagine how Gabe slid it back onto her hand when she was unconscious, especially after she'd promised an imminent wedding. "You're deluded if you think I'm going to make it to a wedding."

"Give the treatment a chance to work." Gabe moved to sit on the edge of the bed. "You'll be back on your feet soon. People go into remission with this stuff all the time."

"You just found out I have leukemia, Gabe." Her tone was rude, but she didn't care. Dying just might finally give her the strength to say what she needed to say. "But I've been dying for a very long time. Now, I said I wanted to speak to my father alone." She lifted her hand and pointed to the door. "Get out."

"What about today like you said? I can find a priest and..."

"Give us a minute, son," her father said, putting a hand on Gabe's chest.

She waited for the door to close behind Gabe before she spoke. "That's what all this is about, isn't it? You want to be able to call him your son. To train him up to be the leader you wanted me to be. So when I'm gone, you won't be alone."

"Is it such a bad thing for a father to want to see his daughter get a happy ending? I'd like to see you settled with a husband who loves you. I think it will help to give you something good to look forward to. So you can get better."

"A happy ending?" She snorted a laugh. "Dad, this is no one's idea of a happy ending. I'm twenty-one, and I'll never see twenty-two. No matter how many chemicals you have the doctors pump into my body. It's too late. I want to go home and die in my own bed. I don't want to spend whatever time I have left inside a hospital room with strangers coming and going all day and night.

"And there is zero chance I will ever marry Gabe, whether I somehow survive this disease or not. You picked the wrong son-in-law. I can't stand him, and I won't wear his ring." Sophie reached for the bedside table where the ring sat. "You can return this for me." She placed the ring in her father's hand.

"I think the stress is getting to you, honey. You were so happy the night we celebrated your engagement." He tried to press the ring back into her hand.

"Dad, I love you, I do." She pushed the ring away. "But sometimes I wonder if you have a selective memory. Don't you remember my reaction to the engagement at all? I screamed at everyone. Told them I was dying. I ran away. Does any of that sound like the behavior of a happy bride?"

"Knock-knock." Someone walked in without knocking at all. "I brought you something I made." Gulliver walked in, and a smile stretched across Sophie's face. She immediately regretted asking the nurse for pain medication that would make her fall asleep soon.

"Gulliver, welcome." Sophie's father stood up to shake Gulliver's hand. "Good to see you again." Claude Devereux clapped him on the back and offered the strange boy his own seat beside Sophie. He loved Gulliver, and for a second, Sophie wished she'd met him a long time ago. Things might have gone differently if there was a boy that both she and her father liked. But then, her father only liked him because he'd been the one to get her to the hospital so quickly when she'd passed out at work. As far as her dad was concerned, Gulliver was a hero, and he trusted him.

"She's a little stressed out today. It's been a hard few days for my girl." Her father stood by her bed, holding her hand. "I have to thank you again for being there for her when she collapsed."

"I'm just glad I was able to help." Gulliver smiled, but there was something odd about him today. Odder than usual.

"I blame the fae." A shadow passed over her father's face. "She didn't get sick until that cursed darkness nearly destroyed our world."

"Dad, kids get leukemia." Sophie yawned, her eyes drooping. "The darkness didn't cause it." She forced a laugh, trying to make light of her father's rantings, but she could tell he was getting worked up and a classic Claude Devereaux lecture was heading their way.

"And we're right back in the hospital because of the stress of the bombing. We have to eliminate these evil creatures from our world, but my Sophie has a tender heart. These battles with the fae are too much for her."

"Did you say you made me something, Gulliver?" Sophie shook off the fog of sleep that wanted to claim her.

"I did." Gulliver smiled.

"I'll leave you two to visit for a little while. Yours is the first visit to put some color back in her face, Gulliver." Her father gave her a sad smile before he left the room.

"I saw something, and it made me think of you." Gulliver searched through the messenger bag at his feet. "I found this really cool rock at the park the other day. It's white with lots of iridescent colors, and it reminded me of those big white flowers that grow in the trees by your cafe."

"The magnolias?" Sophie laughed. "They grow everywhere in New Orleans."

"Well, they remind me of you." Gulliver pulled the stone out of his bag, but it wasn't a stone anymore.

Sophie gasped. "Gullie, you made this?" She took the beautiful magnolia blossom in her hands. The quartz was smooth and a rainbow of colors sparkled in the fluorescent lights.

"It's gorgeous." She turned the flower over in her hands. "You're very talented." She barely had the strength to lift it, so she laid it in her lap. "I'm very tired," she whispered.

"It's okay. I just wanted to bring you this. I hope you feel better soon." A frown marred his face for a moment. "You don't look so good, Sophie. I'm sorry you don't feel well."

"I'm dying, Gullie."

"That doesn't sound good." He leaned forward and touched her arm where the purple and yellow bruises sat as a stark contrast against her pale skin.

"I need to go to sleep now," she murmured.

"I'll just sit here with you for a while. Rest. It'll all be okay soon. I promise."

"Thank you. You're beautiful." She fell asleep with a smile on her face, and Gulliver's gift in her hands.

Chapter Eighteen
GULLIVER

Two days and Gulliver had heard nothing from Toby. Not since their argument. He'd searched the French Quarter from top to bottom but found no trace of Toby or the fae village. He couldn't imagine where Toby and Xavier had gone.

None of the prince's behavior had made any sense since their arrival in the human realm. Really, not since the death of Logan. Gulliver didn't expect Toby to get over the loss of his intended so quickly, but it had been more than six months since the young prince of Eldur had perished on the fire plains. And Toby's wounds were still as fresh as they must have been on that horrible day.

Toby wasn't letting himself grieve properly, and Gulliver didn't know how to help him.

Gulliver tossed and turned restlessly on the narrow bed in the hotel room. For most of his life, he'd never had a room to himself. Even now, as an adult with his own home, his sisters and friends or family were often visiting, and he was rarely alone.

Here in the human realm, without Toby or Tia to keep him sane, and with Sophie fighting for her life in the human healer ward, Gulliver felt more alone than he ever had. The weight of his responsibilities pressed in on him, and he couldn't sleep.

Tia sent him here to help the fae living among the humans, and he was failing miserably. Mostly because he only wanted to help Sophie. He couldn't stop thinking about taking her to the healing pools of Lenya.

"Maybe Toby was right." The pools might not work on a human, but he wanted to try. If the pools could save her life, it was worth her hating him for what he was. He knew she'd never look at him the same again once she saw his true form, but he couldn't bring himself to care.

If only he could open portals. Without Toby's help, Sophie would die. Likely soon. She'd said he was beautiful. Right before she fell asleep. He knew she meant the flower he'd given her was beautiful, but it still made him smile.

Tossing the light blanket aside, Gulliver rolled from the bed to look through the window again. Moonlight illuminated the courtyard outside their room. "Come on, Dad," he whispered in the night, willing his father to hear him, to show up when the sun rose. He was supposed to check on them any day now. Gulliver just hoped it wouldn't be too late for Sophie.

By the next afternoon, Gulliver was frantic. He'd walked the streets of the French Quarter and the surrounding sectors until his feet were blistered and his face was burnt to a crisp from the hot sun that rivaled the unforgiving sun of the Eldurian desert and the Vondurian borderlands where the fire plains once raged.

Sinking down onto the curb, Gulliver let his shoulders droop as he hung his head.

"You come back for that tour, young sir?" A familiar voice had him craning his neck to look behind him. The Voodoo shop.

"I don't suppose you have healing potions in your shop? Or a way to find someone in this overcrowded city?"

The woman's shadow loomed over him, shielding him from the brutal sun. "This person you want healed, is it the same person you want found?" She sat beside him.

"No." Gulliver sighed. "I want to heal my friend Sophie. But to do that, I either need a miracle or to find my friend Toby."

"He's the boy running around the Quarter with Xavier, isn't he?" she muttered into a cloth bag, digging around the contents for something.

"Yes! Have you seen them? I really need to find them."

"You stay away from Xavier. That boy has a kind heart, but he's headed for trouble." She pulled something out of her bag. "Your friend, Sophie, she is sick, yes?"

"She's going to die," Gulliver whispered.

"Maladi Bondye." The woman nodded. "A disease of the Lord."

"I don't know what that means."

"A natural disease, like cancer. It is not always something

magic can heal. Take this. It will not restore her, but it will give her peace as she leaves this world." She held out her hand, smooth and dark like umber.

Gulliver took the odd-shaped pendant.

"It's filled with herbs that will ease her passing. A little bit of this world and some of the world beyond." The woman set her bag on the curb and turned toward him, kindness in her eyes.

"I don't want her to die. I need magic that will save her."

"Sometimes, even magic isn't enough. Good people die every day. This charm will show her the way through the spirit world when she passes. The spirits will recognize her and embrace her."

"Are you fae?" Gulliver took the pendant, tucking it into his pocket. It helped to know if he failed in saving Sophie that he could at least give her this magic.

"Are you?" She gave him a knowing smile. "It is not a good time to admit such things if you are. I hope your friend recovers, but if she doesn't, she will be fine. You might miss her, but the spirits will care for her. She will be happy with them."

"Thank you." Gulliver stood. "I have to go see her." He clutched the pendant in his pocket, searching the sky for traces of the moon. It often rose during the afternoons here, the perfect time for Griffin to visit when he'd have magic in both the fae and human worlds. "I just have to go home to get something first." He took off down the street, hope swelling in his chest. Today would be the day his dad checked in on him. He knew it.

He raced down Esplanade Avenue and skidded to a halt just outside the gates to Lamothe House. It was still afternoon, but the sun would fade soon. Gulliver's heart sank like a stone when he saw no signs of Griff. He crossed the street to sit on a stone bench under the gnarled Cypress trees that looked as though they had been there for as long as New Orleans had.

He sat there for over an hour, just hoping his father would feel how much he needed him. The streets emptied as locals went home to their families and tourists went out to dinner or to the smelly Bourbon Street Gullie avoided as much as possible. The tourists really seemed to like that place. They walked around with drinks in funny-looking glasses Gulliver wanted to try. Though, he didn't hold his drink very well.

Someone sat down beside him, and Gulliver thought about going to get one of those drinks they called a hurricane. He imagined a drink like that could make him forget.

"I see you've been waiting for me." A familiar hand rested on his shoulder. "What's going on, son? You look like you've got the weight of the kingdoms on your shoulders."

"Dad?" Gulliver rubbed his tired eyes. "You're really here?" He lunged for him, letting his father wrap his arms around him.

"I just stepped out of a portal right in front of you, and you didn't flinch." Griffin's arms held him tight. "Tia wanted me to check on you yesterday, but I couldn't get away until just before sunrise this morning. I almost didn't make it." If he'd waited past dawn, he wouldn't have been able to use his magic to open a portal until the moon rose again in the fae realm, which would have coincided with the sun rising here.

"I'm really glad you're here." Gulliver buried his head against Griff's shoulder, his back shaking with relief.

"Come inside and we'll talk about whatever's bothering you. Tia gave me one of her spelled books so you two can communicate. She sent you and Toby here, but I don't think she thought about what that would do to her to have you both gone at the same time. Keir is ... a very patient man." Griffin chuckled. "With a very distracted wife. He asked me to bring you home. Just short of begged, actually."

"I can't go home. Not yet."

"I told him that was not the way to help Tia. She'd just send you right back, and she'd be even more cranky from his attempt to help."

"We don't have much time, Dad. I need to go see Sophie."

"Sophie? Who's Sophie?" Griffin gave his son a long hard look. "Have you met someone?"

"She's a waitress. She's sick. Really sick." Gulliver hopped up from the bench, eager to be off. "I need you to make a portal to Lenya. Tonight."

"Wait, where is Toby?" Griffin pulled him back down on the bench. "Take it easy, Gullie. Start from the beginning and tell me everything."

With an impatient sigh, Gulliver told his father the whole story.

"And you haven't seen Toby since you argued?" Griffin finally spoke when Gulliver finished his hurried explanation.

"No, and if I can't get Sophie to the healing pools in Lenya, or if they don't work for humans, then I at least have a magic token from a voodoo priestess—at least, I think she was a priestess—to help ease her passing."

"And you like this girl? This human girl, who is the

daughter of the man causing so much trouble for our fae here in the human world."

"I don't know how I feel; I just know she is a good person, and she doesn't deserve to die. She's only twenty-one. It's not fair that she has to die when we have the magic that could save her."

"And have you mentioned to this waitress, who brings you the best sweets in the land, that you're fae? That you intend to take her to our world and heal her with magic she doesn't understand?"

"No." Gulliver's shoulders slumped, and his bound tail wanted to thrash in agitation and impatience. "I don't exactly know how to tell her."

"Have you thought about what will happen when you take her to Lenya, where she will see your true features? No one I know has a tail as magnificent as yours, and your mother thinks you have the loveliest eyes of any man she's ever seen, but to humans, those things are strange. She might not react well. At least, not at first."

"I know what you're doing, Dad. And I appreciate it. I know my family loves me and the people who care about me think I'm perfectly handsome and whatever. But the truth is, I am strange. And not just because I have a tail and cat eyes. Or because I'm an orphaned street rat, who happens to be the adopted son of a prince and best friends with a queen. I'm just me, and Sophie seems to like that. If she doesn't care for my tail or eyes ... well, I don't care if she never wants to see me again if it means she gets to live."

"I think you have your answer. You like her. And you might love her enough to risk losing her. Follow your heart, not your head. If risking your heart is worth it, then we have to help this girl. But you have to decide."

"Let's go. She doesn't have much time left."

"We're leaving tonight, then?"

"I think we have to."

Chapter Nineteen
SOPHIE-ANN

You're beautiful. Had she really said that to Gullie's face? Mortified, Sophie tossed and turned, searching for a comfortable position in the horrible hospital bed. That was the bad thing about the medication. She'd slept hard all day, and now she was restless and didn't want any more drugs that would only leave her with a pounding headache and no energy. If she was going to survive a few more days or weeks, she was going to be present for the time her father wanted so desperately.

Even now, he sat beside her, chattering away about HAFS people she really didn't know. But she let him talk. It made him happy. And if she could rally enough, maybe he would even take her home soon.

Though, this time tomorrow, she would be back to asking for something to send her into oblivion. The day after treatments was always the worst.

"Gabe and his boys are working hard to get things ready

for our next big move against the fae. They've really stepped it up this time."

Sophie focused on what her dad was saying. "Another attack?" Her voice came out in hardly more than a whisper. "That's not a good idea when the dust hasn't even settled from the bombing." Her heart raced in her chest as she tried to sit up. "Please don't kill any more people, Dad." The machines beside her began to beep, and she did her best to calm down.

"Hush." He pushed her gently back against her pillows, fussing with her blankets, trying to make her more comfortable when that wasn't possible in her current state. "This time, we have the right intel on the location of one of the biggest fae villages in the entire state. The fae in the city live in scattered neighborhoods, but we found a real village out in the bayou, not too far outside the city. Nothing but fae families as far as you can see, and no humans in sight. This is going to be big, honey. Even the leader of HAFS in New York City is coming down to help us."

"But—"

"We'll talk about it more once you're feeling better. You're going to need your strength back so you can be part of this."

"You and I both know I won't be getting my strength back. Not this time." Her breath came in short gasps, and her father moved to put the oxygen cannula in place so she could breathe better. "Right now, I need you to be my dad and not the leader of HAFS."

"Just rest now." His eyes clouded with worry, and she reached for his hand.

"I need you to promise me one thing."

"Anything." He clasped her hand in his calloused fingers.

"I know we can't allow the fae to use their magic on us. What happened to Mom can never happen again. Their darkness can't be allowed to spread to our world ever again."

"We're going to stop them, baby. I promise."

"No, just listen." She panted; even the oxygen flowing in through her nose wasn't enough. "I need you to promise me that you won't hurt those families. The fae families. The innocents."

"They're not innocents," her father insisted. "They tried to bring eternal darkness to our world. Can you imagine what that would have done to our people? Our world? You don't remember, but in just a few short weeks, everything started dying. We were worried about widespread famine and long-term depression. It was anarchy. People died in the streets. People like your mother. Suicide rates were up. It was hell on Earth."

Sophie glared at him, and he quieted, letting her go on. "But the light returned. Have you ever wondered why that just happened one day? Who knows, maybe they fixed it. There are two sides to every story." Sophie sucked in a breath. "There are good and bad people. Good and bad fae. I'm sure of it. I don't want you to become a bad person, Dad. Make sure the fae you attack are the ones responsible for the darkness and the deaths like Mom's. The others have done nothing but try to live in peace. I need you to let them."

"I—"

"Leave that village alone. Look for the ones who deserve it, and remember ... even for fae ... they should be innocent until proven guilty."

"Looks like someone's having a hard time in here." The night nurse came in, all smiles as she checked Sophie's oxygen and vitals. "She's a little worked up, isn't she?" The nurse smoothed a hand over the faded blue of Sophie's hair. "I'm just going to turn your oxygen up a bit and change you over to a mask to help you catch your breath, but I need you to try to calm down."

Sophie nodded, sitting back and taking a deep breath from the oxygen mask. "Promise me." She held the plastic mask to her face, dragging in another breath.

"I-I promise." He stepped away from the bed, letting the nurse do her job.

"I need you to keep your word."

"Of course. You have my word, and I'll not break it. I just need you to get better so we can make a new plan."

"Do you want something for pain, Sophie, dear?" the nurse asked.

"No. I'm okay." Sophie winced as she shifted onto her side.

"I'll bring you some more pillows when I come back to check on you next. If you're better then, we'll switch you back to the cannula so you can be more comfortable."

"Thanks." Sophie nodded, the rush of oxygen loud in her ears. Whenever the high-flow oxygen mask came into play, it was never a good sign.

"And it sounds like maybe your dad needs a bit of a break too." She eyed Sophie's father. "It might be a good time to go home and get some rest and a good meal, Mr. Devereaux. I'll call you if anything changes."

"She's right, Dad, you need to take care of yourself. I'll be fine. I think I'll watch a movie and maybe play a game on my phone." She would likely just stare at the wall. She didn't have the mental energy for either of those activities, but it would make him feel better.

"All right. I'll call to check on you in a little while." He leaned down to kiss her cheek, and Sophie let out a sigh when he and the nurse left.

It was the thought of all those families living way out in the bayou that changed her mind. It was one thing to attack a cell of fae actively working against the humans, but it was another thing entirely when it came to families with young children. Over the years, Sophie had often wondered where her line in the sand might fall in this war against the fae. Her father had stumbled onto it tonight.

She rolled over, staring at the magnolia blossom on her bedside table. It twinkled back at her in the dim glow of the nightlight, and it made her smile to think that Gulliver—kind, sweet, strange Gulliver—had made it for her simply because the flower reminded him of her.

No. You're young. Even humans don't die this young. It's a lie.

His words had come back to her at some hazy point earlier in the day when the chemicals in her body started to work. She didn't really feel better. Not yet, but it was a familiar feeling, as if her body might rally one last time. But she knew for certain it wouldn't last long. When she'd felt like this before, she'd had months, sometimes even years of feeling better. This time it would be days. Perhaps long enough to see him again before she went home to die.

Gulliver. The nice man who said the oddest things, had the biggest sweet tooth she'd ever seen, and wouldn't hurt a fly. The man who made her smile whenever he walked into the cafe. The one who talked of healing herbs, plastic money, and feletisions. The one she just might have fallen for if she'd had a little more time.

Chapter Twenty
GULLIVER

"What about Toby?" Griffin followed Gulliver along Esplanade Avenue to the trolley stop. "We can't just leave him in the city by himself."

"Toby will be fine." Gulliver's long strides quickened as they neared the stop. The trolley would be along in a few minutes, and he didn't want to miss it.

"We'll come back for him after we help Sophie. You're more familiar with Lenya than I am. Once we find Sophie, I'll open a portal for you, but I'll stay here to look for Toby. He's a grown man, but Brea would never forgive me for leaving him here in his current state."

"He seems to be doing better in some ways." Gulliver rushed across the street to the small covered station where the streetcar waited to take them through the Quarter. "In other ways, he's still not dealing well with Logan's death." Gulliver took the two steps onto the trolley and slipped into a seat at the back of the empty car.

"Which is why we can't leave him behind." Griffin sat beside him, looking over his shoulder. "This is a strange sort of automobile, isn't it?"

"They call it a trolley or a streetcar. Either way, it will take us close to the Tulane Medical Center. It's supposed to be a very good place for healing."

"Shouldn't we let the humans treat her illness? Their potions and medicines can take much longer than ours to work, but wouldn't it be for the best?"

Gulliver shook his head. "They say they don't have anything left to give her. Just herbs to keep her comfortable until she dies."

"That seems wrong." Griffin clutched the grab bar in front of him as the trolley picked up speed.

"Canal Street!" the driver called as they neared the end of the route.

"We'll get off here." Gulliver stood as the car rolled to a stop, and they exited to the busy intersection.

"I don't think I like trollies." Griffin followed Gulliver across the street, matching his stride to Gulliver's pace.

"You get used to them. I like it better than taxis. You're less likely to abduct someone when you know where all the trollies stop."

"You're going to have to explain what accidental abductions you've made when we have more time."

"It's easier than you think." Gulliver guided them down Canal Street to Tulane Avenue and the large brick building that housed the healers.

"This is it?" Griffin stared up at the large square building. "It looks like something from the prison world before the barrier came down."

"Depressing, isn't it?" Gulliver stared up at the rows of dark windows. "Sophie has so much light in her. I can't bear to think of her dying in such a terrible place."

"How do we get in?"

"I tried to come see her last night, but they yelled at me when I walked into the building. Something about it being after visiting hours."

"We'll have to sneak in." Griffin tapped him on the shoulder. "Perhaps we can find a door back there?" He pointed to a dark alley between the medical center and another building.

They crept down the alley, where large garage doors seemed to be locked up tight. He wasn't sure how anyone could drive a car through those doors as high up as they were.

"It says this is the loading docks," Griffin whispered. "No public access. I think that means we're not supposed to be here."

"Let's try that door over there behind those big green bins." He'd seen plenty of those things in the city. It was where the humans put their garbage, and they had a lot of it.

"Locked." Griffin pushed his shoulder against the door, but it wouldn't budge. He turned and looked down the alley before he ducked back into the shadows.

"Wait!" But Gulliver didn't have time to stop him before the purple light of his magic illuminated the door and it opened.

Griffin smiled, holding the door open for him.

"You have to be careful here, Dad. HAFS is always watching for any signs of magic." Gulliver darted into the dark room.

"Are they everywhere?"

"We don't know." Gulliver closed the door behind them. "Just be more careful about using your magic while you're here. I'm serious; it's not safe."

"Correct me if I'm wrong, but aren't we here to save a girl using my magic portals?" Griffin searched the wall for a light switch.

"Just don't use your magic unless there is literally no other choice."

"Fine." Griffin found a switch, and the room flooded with bright light. It was a kitchen.

"They make food here?" Griffin seemed bewildered by that.

"Not very good food, I can tell you that much. People like Sophie have to stay here for days and days to get their healing potions, so they have to feed them. But sometimes, I wonder if it's the food making her so sick. It's really awful."

"This coming from the boy who would eat anything. It must be bad."

"We need to find a way out of here." Gulliver pushed through a swinging door and relief flooded him. "It's the dining hall. I've been here before." He waved Griffin over, and they made their way across the hall to the locked doors.

"Want me to open them?" Griffin asked.

"No. The lock is on this side." Gulliver turned the latch and pushed through the double doors, peeking into the main corridor of the medical center. It was quiet. "Let's go. We can catch the elevators down the hallway."

Outside of the dining hall, the way was clear, but the lights were dim and a thick rope closed off the area.

"What's that?" Griffin walked past a window filled with pastries and sandwiches.

"They call it the coffee cart. The food is much better there than in the dining hall, but they don't take plastic money. And they really don't like it when you order a lot and then don't have the paper money to pay for it."

"Hey, what are you doing back there? The cafeteria is closed!" A bright light flashed in Gulliver's eyes, and he couldn't see anything. Throwing his hands up to shield his eyes, he called out, "We were just looking for the elevators, sir."

"It's after hours. You shouldn't be here." The security guard marched toward them. "And you shouldn't be back there. Didn't you see that the area is closed to guests? Are you trying to steal something?"

"No, my good man," Griffin said in his most princely voice. "My son and I were here earlier today visiting a friend, and he lost his plastic money card."

"I see." The guard relaxed his stance. "I'm afraid you'll have to leave. You can come back in the morning to find your credit card."

"It's really important that I find it." Gulliver took a step back from the officer. "We'll just be a minute." Gulliver ducked behind the coffee cart, and that seemed to be the worst thing to do.

"All right, you two. Come with me." The guard grabbed Gulliver's arm and hauled him and Griffin down the hall. He was very strong for a human.

The man marched them to the front entrance and shoved them through the magic doors and onto the sidewalk.

"Come back when the hospital is open, or if you have to be here, stay in the emergency room area only."

The magic doors slid shut, and Gulliver sank down onto the curb. They needed to get to Sophie tonight. Griffin's night magic wouldn't work tomorrow, and then they'd be back in the same situation tomorrow night, unable to enter the building.

"What's that he said about the emergency room?" Griffin asked.

"I think that's where they take the really sick people who need immediate attention."

"Is that it over there?" Griffin pointed to a sign they'd missed earlier. Bright red with glowing white letters, Gulliver wasn't sure how he'd missed it before.

"Looks like it's just over there." Gulliver stood, brushing off his pants and following his father down the sidewalk and around the corner.

"Oh. This looks promising," Griffin said. "You think you can pretend to be sick?"

Gulliver's brows shot up in surprise as he realized what his father was suggesting. "I do think I'm feeling a bit peaky. Plus, all those humans on TV are always sick and telling me I might be too." He coughed, hunching his shoulders as they neared the magic doors. Here, the lights were bright and the waiting room filled with people.

"You can act human, right?" Griffin whispered at the last minute.

"I've been doing it for weeks." Gulliver shuffled up to the counter, where a frazzled-looking nurse sorted through a pile of folders on her desk.

"Help me!" Gulliver crashed into the counter. "I have the mesothelioma!" He sucked in a breath, choking and gasping. "It's bad, nurse. Oh, nurse, I can't breathe. My chest ... hurts." He clutched his heart and collapsed.

"Help my son!" Griffin cried. "He needs a healer now!"

"Oh my, he's not breathing." The nurse rushed out to the waiting room with a wheelchair, and Gulliver groaned, making his body go limp as she maneuvered him into the chair.

"You his father?" she asked.

"Yes. Please help him. He's all I have left of his mother!" Griffin sprinted behind her, letting out a sob as she called for a doctor.

"We'll get him in triage." She wheeled him into a room, pulling the curtain shut behind her. "He's breathing now." She grabbed a funny-looking device and shoved the stems into her ears.

"That's cold!" Gulliver whimpered as she pressed a flat disc against his chest. "It hurts! Oh, it's like knives stabbing my lungs."

"Shhh. We'll take care of you." She helped Gulliver stand, moving him onto the bed. "Your heartrate is high. Can you take a deep breath for me, son?" She grabbed another weird-looking device and wrapped it around Gulliver's arm.

"It hu-rts ... too much ... to breathe."

She pushed a button, and the thing around Gulliver's arm swelled, gripping his arm in a painful vise.

"Ouch! That really hurts!" His eyes widened in alarm. That really did hurt. "What's she doing?" It felt like she was trying to amputate his arm. "It's my lungs, not my arm, lady."

"Relax, I just need to take your blood pressure."

"She wants to take my blood? You can't do that!" Gulliver tried to lunge from the bed, but Griffin pushed him back down.

"Relax, Gul. Let her work, and then she'll go get the doctor."

"Did he say he has mesothelioma?" she asked, her torture device cutting off Gulliver's circulation. "He's awfully young for it. Does he work construction?"

"Yes. It's my fault." Griffin ran a hand through his hair. "I've always worked construction since he was a little kid."

"I see." She frowned. "He's awfully thin. How long has he been experiencing symptoms?"

"Uh, a few weeks," Griffin said.

"Weeks? And you're just now bringing him in?"

"He's a grown man living on his own. I, uh, came to visit and found him like this."

"Good thing you brought him in. His BP and pulse are dangerously high, but he's breathing on his own. I'll send the doctor in right away, and we'll get figure out what's going on."

"Can I get a room? On the fourth floor?" Gulliver asked. That was where Sophie was.

She nodded. "You've been here before, haven't you? We'll get you settled if we decide you need to stay, and the doctors will run some tests to see what we're dealing with. I'll be right back with something that will help you get your breath under control."

"Thank you." Griffin followed her to the curtain. "I don't know what I'd do without him."

"We'll take good care of him, sir."

"Thank you!" Griffin closed the curtain behind her, and Gulliver leaped out of the bed. "What was that thing she put on my arm? I can hardly feel it." He clutched his arm against his chest.

"What the heck is mesothelioma, and how did you know what to say?"

"Saw it on TV. It's a terrible disease people get, and the man on TV says I can get a lot of money as compensation for it. I mean, if I really had it. He's on TV a lot during the day, so I imagine lots of humans have it."

"Quick thinking. You were very convincing." Griffin peeked through the curtain. "Let's hurry before she comes back with whatever that thing was she mentioned. I don't think you want that if it's like what she used to remove your blood. Are you okay?" Griffin examined his arm.

"Fine now that it's not squeezing the life out of me."

"Okay, let's go that way. Looks like there's a door we can use to get away from the nurse with the scary contraptions. What was that thing she put in her ears? Did it hurt?" Griffin led them down the quiet hall to the door.

"No, it was just really cold. Not sure what it did to my chest." Gulliver tugged his shirt and looked down at the smooth skin of his chest. "Seems fine."

"It's a room with stairs." Griffin stared at the steps that seemed to lead to nowhere.

"It should take us to the fourth floor, shouldn't it?" Gulliver rushed up the first flight and called back down to Griffin. "It says second floor up here."

Griffin took the steps two at a time to reach him, and

they made their way to the door with a sign for the fourth floor. It was the cancer wing.

"Shh." Griffin peeked through the door into the long hallway. "Look familiar?"

"She's in room 467." Gulliver stepped into the hall. "The sign there says this is for rooms 440 to 470. This is it." Gulliver picked up his pace, skidding to a stop outside her door.

"She's sleeping." Griffin peered through the narrow window, carefully opening the door.

Quietly, they crossed the room. The only sound was the beeping of the machines and the rush of air from the tube in Sophie's nose.

"She looks so fragile." Griffin stepped to her bedside. "Are you sure about this?"

Gulliver nodded. "Positive." He watched her sleeping, the magnolia he'd carved for her clutched in her hand.

"She has blue hair? I didn't think humans had things like blue hair."

"Me either, but I think it's beautiful."

"Well, grab your girl and let's go."

Gulliver hiked his bag higher on his shoulder and leaned forward to remove the tube from her nose and the needle from her arm. He hoped he was doing it right but there was no time to second-guess the decision. He tried not to hurt her before lifting her into his arms.

Griffin already had the portal open, and Gulliver could see the sunny castle grounds of the one place he swore he'd never return. Vondur, though it was known simply as Lenya now.

"Good luck, Gullie. I'll come to check on you as soon as I

find Toby." Griffin reached through the portal to grasp his shoulder. "I hope your girl makes it."

"Thanks, Dad." Gulliver cradled Sophie's head against his chest and stepped into the portal. He turned around before it closed. "And be careful!" But the portal closed before Gulliver had a chance to tell him anything else he needed to know.

Chapter Twenty-One
GULLIVER

"Wha—" Sophie tried to lift her head, but it dropped back over Gulliver's arm. Her chest rose with raspy breaths that seemed to take a great deal of effort.

She was cold, her skin damp with sweat. Soft murmurs escaped her lips, but no full sentences. Her eyes remained shut as Gulliver sprinted toward the palace, where he once was held captive. The palace where a noose once slid over his head. He could still feel the rope burning into the skin of his neck.

This place wasn't the same. Vondur no longer existed, melding with Grima to become one kingdom under the rule of Queen Bronagh. And still, it held only nightmares for him.

The fire plains closing in, fleeing to the mountains above Grima.

The walls still held signs of the battle with the vatlands,

black scorch marks stretching across stone and mortar. A new wooden gate now replaced the one that had held out enemy armies for many years. Unlike before, it stood open, a welcome to visitors who stopped by to see the current residents of the castle.

Gulliver wouldn't be welcome once they learned of his request. No, he wouldn't request the use of the healing pools. He'd demand it. He never asked the Lenyans for a single thing after everything he suffered at their hands. They owed him this.

"Gul ..." Sophie tried to say his name, but she couldn't seem to get it out. Her lids opened slowly like doors on rusted hinges, and her eyes were cloudy, as if she no longer saw the world.

"Shhh." He shifted her in his arms. "I'm going to save you, Sophie-Ann Devereaux. I promise. You're not dying today." The magic had to work on humans. If it didn't, what was the point? Fae, human, it didn't matter. Their power was meant to help those who needed it, to make the worlds better places.

How would any world improve by losing such a bright soul?

His legs ached as he finally reached the gate and skidded to a halt. A line of soldiers in Vondurian red greeted him. They didn't draw their weapons, but they didn't need to.

Gulliver's breath wheezed as he tried to calm his heart. "I ... need ..." He looked down at Sophie, at the way she stared at the cloudless sky motionlessly, still. Dead.

"No." The words were only for her. "Don't die on me." A tear slid down his face. "It isn't your time." He lifted his gaze to the soldiers as one of them stepped forward.

"We saw the portal open. Do you have word from Iskalt?" There was distrust in his voice, suspicion in his gaze. Gulliver was used to such treatment with his appearance.

He tightened his jaw, lifting his chin. "Bring Lady Eavha to me. I have a friend in need of a kind of help only this palace can provide. She will know where I am."

He tried to bull through them, but the fae in charge lifted a hand to use his magic, most likely to bind Gulliver to the spot. "You will wait for her here."

"No." Gulliver's defensive magic threw up a shield around both him and Sophie. "I will not."

Again, the guard tried to hold him in place with his power. There was no time for this. Anger ripped through Gulliver. Anger at Sophie's illness, at Toby for keeping him from bringing her here days ago, at these guards who wasted precious moments that could be the difference between saving her life or losing the one person who truly saw him.

A burst of defensive Myrkurian magic exploded out of him, reflecting the guard's own power. Gulliver saw the moment the fae went stiff, his rapidly blinking eyes the only part of him not frozen in place.

Sophie didn't move in his arms. Not even her chest rose with signs of life.

"This isn't happening." He charged past the rest of the guards, who only watched him in shock. The palace looked different after the repairs, but the layout was the same. He rushed through the halls, ignoring servants yelling after him, others jumping out of his way.

"Stay with me, Soph." His arms had long gone numb from carrying her, but nothing would stop him. He kicked in the door to the old sitting room and went straight for the opening to the tunnels. It was secret to most fae, but he wasn't most fae.

Sophie's toes scraped the damp wall as he hurried farther and farther into the heart of the castle. Giant caverns spread out before him, crystals sparkling in the walls, their magic now in their beauty rather than any real power.

Gulliver's heavy steps echoed in the damp space. His own breath sounded like a roaring in his ears. A bubbling sound grew louder as he neared the wide pools that held the magic of a thousand crystals crushed into the stone. They held the most powerful magic in all the kingdoms, healing even the gravest of wounds.

Yet, they did not bring a soul back to life.

Could they cure a disease?

"Gulliver, stop." Eavha ran into the cavern, her giant cat, Sheeba, loping behind her. They both skidded to a halt. "You can't do this."

"Don't come any closer, Eavha." He stared down into the frothing water. "I can't let her die."

"That's not your decision to make."

He didn't look at her, couldn't. "And whose is it? Who gets to choose those worthy enough to save? You and Declan? Do you know how hard it is for me to set foot in this castle?"

"I do."

"Then, you know how much Vondur owes me."

"Of course we do, and if that were a fae in your arms, I would help lower her into the water myself, but she's human; I can see it from here. We don't know what it would do to her. They aren't the same as us. What if it only prolongs her pain? Would you do that to her? Have you even given her a choice?"

He choked back his tears. "What if it doesn't? I can save her."

"Gul—"

"No. I care about you, Eavha, and I'm scared of Declan, so I won't insult you by calling out your fear of humans—"

"You just did."

"But I'm not scared." If Sophie survived this, she'd wake up, see his true self, and despise him. Yet, he wasn't afraid. Not this time. "We keep ourselves so separate from humans and claim they are not like us, but you do not know them. You don't know her. She deserves a chance to live."

Sheeba growled, but Eavha put a hand on her head to quiet her as Gulliver looked back over his shoulder. "Your guards can drag me away after." He lowered Sophie to the ground, gently cradling her head until it rested against the stone and let the canvas bag hanging over one shoulder thump to the ground beside her. "Throw me back in those horrid dungeons." He sat on the edge, not bothering to remove his shoes or clothes before sliding into the pool. "I'll go through it all again as long as I save her first."

The warm water enveloped him, wrapping him in a layer of magic that buzzed along his skin. All weariness faded away, any ache in his limbs was gone. His tail rose to the surface, flicking the water. His feet scrambled for a steady footing on the loose bottom, covered by fresh layers of crushed crystals.

Wrapping his hands around Sophie's ankles, he pulled her toward him. When it grew easier to move her, he looked up to find Eavha pushing her shoulders. "You're right." She met his gaze. "We have to try."

Keir's sister had always been Gulliver's favorite Lenyan, but he'd forever remember the kindness and gentleness she showed him now. Even Sheeba shoved Sophie with her nose, trying to help.

"Thank you."

Eavha smiled. "You love her, Gullie. That means I do too."

Love. Did he love her? The only love he'd ever known was for his adoptive family, for Tia. This wasn't like that, yet the thought of losing Sophie sent him plummeting into the darkness not unlike what Toby currently found himself in.

Sophie's body slipped the rest of the way into the water, and he caught her against him, looking down into her pale face. It wasn't long ago she smiled at him for the first time, and it stole the air from his lungs. He saw the signs now, thinking back on each interaction. Through all that time, she'd been suffering, just trying to get through her days, trying to survive as long as she could.

"If I'd known, I could have saved her earlier." He brushed wet hair back from her cheeks. There were no signs of life, no movement in her chest or flushing of the skin.

Sophie was as cold as she'd been before he brought her into the warm water.

Eavha lowered herself to the edge of the rough-cut pool that was hewn right into the rock generations ago. She dangled her feet over the edge, ignoring the fact that water soaked into the bottom of her gown.

"I'm sorry, Gullie." Her face said everything he needed to know.

It should have worked by now.

He shook his head. "There's still time."

Eavha gave him a sympathetic look that on anyone else might have resembled pity. Not with her. The empathetic Lady of Vondur truly cared that he was hurting. "What was her ailment?"

"The humans called it cancer." He couldn't stop staring down at Sophie's still form as he clutched her to him. This couldn't be the end. Tears slipped down his cheeks. "She didn't even get to live, not really." Under her father's thumb, she'd never experienced the good in life. Only fear, hatred, darkness. She died not knowing who he truly was.

Eavha sighed. "There is so much we don't know about these pools. They may not know what to do with human ailments."

"I promised her." He wasn't sure Sophie had heard him, but it didn't matter. He'd said the words, told her he'd save her. His chest shook with silent sobs.

Eavha sniffled and wiped her eyes. "I wish this could have worked for you."

Keir would have guarded the pools more staunchly. Declan probably would have followed his friend's rule. Most fae he knew wouldn't take a risk to save a human, but Eavha wasn't like most. She reminded him of Tia. He thought of the book in his bag that would let him contact his best friend and tell her he needed her.

Gulliver wasn't sure what made him do it, but he pressed the voodoo charm into her hand and released Sophie, letting her sink into the pool. He closed his eyes for a brief moment, picturing her as the kind girl he'd met in a cafe in the weirdest city he'd ever seen. She grounded him when his mission left him so alone. And now, she was gone.

He hoped the voodoo priestess was right. "The spirits are guiding you now." He pulled himself onto the ledge to sit beside Eavha, letting tears run unashamed down his cheeks. "I tried."

She reached over, taking his hand. "She knew that."

His shoulders shook, and Eavha slid an arm across his back, pulling him down to rest his head on her shoulder. "What was her name?"

"Sophie-Ann." He closed his eyes.

"Tell me about her."

He drew in a breath. "Well, for starters, she hated the fae." And then, he told her everything. All of it. Leaving nothing out. When he was finished, there was nothing left inside of him. No tears, no more stories. He was a hallowed husk of a fae.

For the first time, he truly understood Toby. It was not a lesson he'd ever wanted to learn.

Chapter Twenty-Two

SOPHIE-ANN

Sophie floated through space, unable to grasp anything to slow the momentum, unable to break free of the darkness surrounding her.

Her entire body burned. Muscles contracting and lengthening too quickly, veins pulsing as her head hammered rapidly. Heat seared through each organ, every blood vessel. She wanted to scream, to tell someone, anyone, to stop the agony.

Had she died? She'd been so sure it was the end. Staring at a sky that was somehow too blue, unnaturally painted against a barren landscape she didn't recognize, she'd said her final farewells, readied herself for God.

Her body writhed as the scorching wave washed up through her abdomen, inflating her lungs and filling the cavity around her heart with a feeling she couldn't decipher.

Power. She felt powerful as she bore the agony, as her body broke and healed and burned from the inside out.

She opened her mouth to speak, and water flooded it, traveling down her windpipe and into her lungs. She coughed, and more water streamed in. Which way was up?

When she pried her eyes open, all she saw was the brilliant glittering sand that brushed her toes. It was the most magnificent sight she'd ever seen. Was she on her way to heaven?

If so, she was ready. Her time on Earth was finished, and she'd soon join her mother. Maybe she'd finally find peace.

A voice, muffled by the water, yelled something that sounded like, "Eve, look!"

Eve? A hazy part of her brain wondered if it was *the* Eve.

Water splashed around her, and large hands gripped under her arms, pulling her to the surface.

"I swear I saw her move." A man's voice. God?

"You're only seeing what you want to see," the woman said, sadness in her tone. "I'm sorry, but she's gone. We can't bring her back."

Another wave of pain hit her, slithering along her skin until her head broke the surface. She sucked air into her lungs, staring up at the man and woman who were no longer looking at her.

"We should prepare her body." The woman bowed her head. "You know it's all we have left. Do you wish to bring her back to the humans?"

"Don't you dare tell me to give up hope, Eavha. I know what I saw. She moved in that water."

Sophie's eyes were closed now. She couldn't bear the torchlight or the shining of whatever gems these walls held. There was no more strength left in her. Her entire body ached with remnants of a pain she didn't understand, but she managed to draw breath into her lungs, something she'd struggled with for days.

"Just help me get her out." The man sounded familiar, but she couldn't place his voice. It was too rough with emotion. "Coming to Vondur was a waste of her remaining strength. Maybe human medicine would have been a better route."

"I tried to tell you that," the woman said, "but you wouldn't listen."

"Nothing good ever happens in this castle. I shouldn't have expected this time to be different." He wiped a hand across his eyes.

"Give me a break, Gulliver. It's not the same here as it used to be, and you know it."

Gulliver? Sophie wanted to reach out to him, to make him tell her what was going on. But she couldn't move her arms. They were frozen, held down by exhaustion. She couldn't remember ever feeling this drained of energy.

Gulliver held Sophie just above the water, her short hair fanned out over one arm. It felt like a living thing atop her head, writhing with power.

I'm okay, she wanted to say. *I'm right here*. But the words wouldn't come. How was she there?

Had the treatment finally helped? Was her father getting the news from the doctor that she was still alive? She'd felt herself fading from the world, felt the world fading from her.

But now, it was back in full, painful focus. *I wanted to leave*. She hated that thought but couldn't help it. *Why couldn't they let me go?* It was still just a matter of time. She was dying, and each treatment only gave her a short time, if any at all. *Let me be at peace*. "Please," she whispered.

Neither Gulliver nor the woman heard her. A tear trickled from her eye, mingling with the water warming her cheeks.

Something brushed her arm, but she didn't see what it was, only felt the comfort it tried to provide her. It was soft, like the end of a brand new paintbrush. It wrapped over her back, comforting in its embrace.

She should have been afraid that something was in the water. A snake, maybe? Instead, calm flooded her, overpowering the pain, the fear. Her eyes opened halfway.

"Eavha." Grief laced the single word.

The woman didn't respond, but she pulled her legs from the water, ringing out the bottom of a beautiful dark purple dress with black gems sewn into the hem. She looked like she belonged in a different era, with dark curls tumbling down over her ears and across her shoulders. She wore a simple carved heart necklace that looked like it was made of the same stone as that on her dress.

This woman, this ... Eavha ... she looked like a princess straight from a storybook.

Teeth grazed Sophie's shoulder before latching onto the collar of the hospital gown and pulling. Sophie looked up into the eyes of an animal that belonged in a zoo, with barriers between it and the humans. She wanted to scream, but her throat closed up, and she couldn't even breathe.

Eavha pulled her toward the lip of the pool, and rough stone scraped her back, bare where the gown opened. She didn't have time to be embarrassed by her state of dress, by the way the sopping garment clung to her frail body. The cool floor made her want to stay in the warm water.

Her eyes met the other woman's, and Eavha's mouth fell open. She clapped both hands across it.

Gulliver pulled himself from the pool, and Sophie's gaze found him. But it wasn't him at all.

A beast stood in his place.

Her entire body seized as she finally found her voice, her scream echoing through the giant cavern she found herself trapped in.

Chapter Twenty-Three
GULLIVER

Sophie's screams tore right through Gulliver, and he screamed with her. Their voices bounced off the stone walls, and Eavha pressed her hands over her ears.

He crouched beside her, so surprised and overjoyed to see her beautiful eyes bright and alive … and frightened. He hadn't realized through his elation that Sophie was utterly terrified, but he couldn't seem to stop screaming.

"Wait," he gasped, reaching for her hand. Sophie pulled away, scrambling back across the cavern floor as far as she could get. "What are we screaming about?" His heart plummeted at the look of horror on her face. His shouts had been from relief that she wasn't dead, and for a moment, he'd thought hers were the same and they were celebrating together.

Sophie gaped at him, her cries fading to whimpers.

"It's okay, Sophie. You're going to be fine now." His voice

faded, and he fell back, unable to meet her gaze.

"Your eyes," she whispered. "You have a tail!" Sophie's voice shook with something akin to revulsion.

The tail in question snaked up over his shoulder, and Gulliver clutched it to his chest. "Well, it's a really good tail."

"Gullie," Eavha approached where he sat on the cold stone floor, "we should get her into some dry clothes. Both of you."

"Let me help you." Gulliver moved slowly to help Sophie, but she seemed to shrink into herself, hiding among the shadows of the cavern. "It's just me." He waited patiently for her to take his hand, but her eyes grew frantic as she searched for a way around him.

"Hi there, Sophie." Eavha moved to stand between Sophie and Gulliver. "My name is Eavha. You're going to be just fine, though I'm sure you have lots of questions. Can I help you up to one of our guest rooms in the palace? It's much nicer than these old caves. And I promise we'll get you home safely very soon. Gullie here is such a gentle soul. He couldn't bear to see you suffer, so he brought you to the one place that could help you. And the healing pools seem to have worked. How do you feel?"

Gulliver backed away from Sophie while Eavha did what she could to set her at ease. Eavha was a beautiful young fae woman whose only distinctly fae features were her delicately pointed ears. She was much less alarming than Gulliver was himself.

He watched as Sophie finally nodded and took Eavha's hand, pulling herself up from the dusty floor. It was worth every risk Gulliver had taken to get her here.

"I do feel ... better. I think," Sophie said in a soft whisper.

Water streamed from her body as she stood, leaving her hospital gown clinging to her and nearly transparent. Gulliver averted his eyes but gasped as every drop of water fell to the floor, collecting in a puddle before it ran back into the pool in a steady stream. Sophie was still damp, but mostly dry, and her gown now hung loosely around her.

"We are more powerful now, thanks to Tierney," Eavha explained. "The healing crystals have been replenished, and this place is far more magical and unpredictable than it has ever been."

Sophie let out a startled gasp, covering her mouth in surprise as she studied Eavha.

"Magic is just a word, dear Sophie. No need to fear it. I promise." She took Sophie's hand and led her from the caverns and through the palace walls she knew so well.

Gulliver followed, leaving a careful distance between himself and Sophie. He couldn't stand to see the fear and revulsion in her eyes when she looked at him. He'd expected this, knew it would happen, yet it still hurt to see her rejection. Her fear of his strange features.

"Here we are." Eavha led them into a guest room Gulliver had never seen before.

"We're in the west wing, Gullie. The royal residence is the only part of the palace we use now. The east wing, where you've stayed before, has been opened to the refugees of Lenya. All who have lost their homes or livelihoods to the fire plains have a place here or in the old Grima palace with our new queen. At least until we finish rebuilding. We've recovered so much new territory that was lost to the burning lands. It's been an exciting time here in Lenya." She swept around the room, opening curtains to let the light in, fluffing pillows, and checking the linens. "Isn't Lenya such a wonderful word?" She danced around in a circle. "You won't believe just how much our kingdom has changed since we've united under a single banner."

"What is a Lenya?" Sophie turned to Gulliver for answers. "I don't think I understood a single thing she just said."

Gulliver smiled, relieved to hear a bit of the old Sophie in her voice. "Lenya is a where, not a what." He took a hesitant step closer, pausing when she seemed to tremble at his presence. "I've brought you to the fae world. I'm sorry it was such a hasty decision, and that I didn't give you a choice." He ducked his head, shoving his hands in his pockets to appear less threatening. "You were dying. There wasn't enough time. Bringing you to the kingdom of Lenya was the only thing I could do to help. The healing pools ... I didn't even know if it would work on a human, but I had to try. I couldn't let you die in that cold, awful place all alone, knowing there was a chance you could live."

"And your ... friend?" She looked at Eavha.

"She's the best fae you'll ever meet." Gulliver smiled. "Though there are plenty more that are kind and generous too." He shuffled his feet, his tail flicking furiously behind him. "Not all of us are bad," he whispered to his feet as he grabbed his tail. "You're completely safe here."

"I'll have my maid bring you some tea and refreshments in a moment." Eavha flipped the covers back. "But let's get you settled in bed. The healing will make you very tired, and you'll need to sleep for quite some time. I imagine as a human, you will need even more rest before you are fully restored."

"I am very tired." Sophie yawned. "It almost seems like I'm asleep and I'm just dreaming." She took a step toward the bed.

"I'll bring you something comfortable to sleep in." Eavha moved to the armoire beside the bed and searched for a nightdress. "You can change in the bathing chamber." She opened a narrow door in the corner of the room.

"Oh. It's a bathroom." Sophie's legs trembled as she made her way across the room, closing the door behind her.

"She didn't know anything about the fae world?" Eavha whirled around, hands on hips. "Gullie, you know better than to bring a human here like this!"

"I don't care. It worked."

"Bron and Tia will have your tail for this. You know that, right?"

Gulliver shrugged. "I'll do my best to explain myself to them." He sank down onto the edge of the bed. "I had to save her."

"You should have asked for permission from the rulers of the five kingdoms. The healing pools have grown more powerful since new crystals were added. Everyone from Myrkur to Eldur and beyond would be desperate to have access to what you just took."

"It's better to ask for forgiveness than permission when a life is on the line. Even if that life is human."

Eavha sat down beside him. "Can she be trusted?"

"I don't know," he answered honestly. "But if it were Declan, what would you have done?"

Eavha snorted a laugh. "The exact same thing." She reached for him, smoothing a hand across his cheek just as Sophie opened the door of the bath chamber. Her face was pale, and she looked exhausted as she gripped the door to keep from falling.

"I don't think my legs work."

"Sophie." Gulliver darted to her side and lifted her into his arms. "You need to rest." He moved to lay her on the bed, tucking the frilly white nightdress around her before he settled the blankets over her.

She didn't say anything, but she didn't shy away from him either. He'd take that for a win.

"We will let you get some sleep." Eavha laid a hand on Gulliver's arm. "When you wake, there will be refreshments on your bedside table. If you need anything, just ring for the maid." She showed Sophie how to pull the golden silk cord hanging from the wall by the bed. "It will ring downstairs, and Ariella will come to check on you. She is discrete enough not to let the whole palace know we have a human guest."

"I'll come by to check on you later." Gulliver followed Eavha to the door, unable to tear his eyes from Sophie. She was so tired that it scared him. Maybe the pools hadn't healed her after all. What if she died while he was gone? He didn't want her to have to die alone.

"She will be fine, Gullie. It's just the cost of healing. It makes any fae more tired than they have ever been. Sophie is human, so we just need to give her time to sleep it off."

Gulliver nodded, moving to close the door behind them.

"Gullie," Sophie sighed his name.

"Yes?" He leaned back into the room. "What do you need?"

"My father is going to kill you for this."

Chapter Twenty-Four
SOPHIE-ANN

Sophie stirred under the soft, cool sheets, finer than anything she'd ever slept in. She didn't want to open her eyes and break the spell of the best sleep she'd ever had. Stretching under the covers, she relished the comfortable bed as the last vestiges of sleep left her and reality started to catch up.

"What the heck?" She sat up straight, glancing around the small but elegant room. The soft supple blanket was a pale dove gray wool with fancy embroidered flowers around the top.

"Not dead." She patted her hands down the odd nightgown she didn't remember putting on. It was the kind grandmas everywhere wore, but Sophie had never worn a nightgown in her life.

She looked around the room. A thick carpet in shades of blush and pearl covered the floor, and the large windows sported long drapes in a sparkling silver fabric tied back with ropes of pearls. It was a room fit for a princess in a fairy castle.

Sophie sucked in a breath as she looked out the window to the rolling green lawns and puffy white clouds painted across blue skies. Mountains rose in the distance. She was clearly not in New Orleans anymore.

"Gullie." She scooted to the edge of her bed, thoughts of the previous night flooding her mind. The healing pool. Eavha and her pointed ears. "Gullie has a tail." A hand came up to her mouth as she gasped. She was in a place called Lenya. In the fae realm.

And she felt great. Better than she'd felt in a decade. But she was in the fae world with no idea how to get home. Her dad would be frantic, and if he ever found out Gullie was fae and that he'd brought her to the fae world—even if it had been to heal her—he would kill him before he had a chance to explain.

She had to go. She had to find her clothes and figure out how to get home. Sophie lurched out of the bed and stumbled to a stop. A scream welled up in her throat, and she grabbed a pillow from the bed, clutching it in front of her for protection from the huge cat sitting on its haunches between Sophie and the door.

The cat stared at her with a predator's eyes, and Sophie couldn't breathe as it yawned, showing off fanged teeth and powerful jaws.

"Please don't eat me," Sophie whispered as she backed toward the bathroom, holding her pillow out like a shield. "I'm human, and we're really gross. You don't want to bother with me in particular. I'm full of powerful medications that turn my insides to goo. You won't like the taste at all."

"Sheeba, shoo." Eavha swept into the room carrying a tea tray.

Sophie gasped as she gave the huge cat a shove with her foot.

"You shouldn't be scaring our guest. It's not polite. I'm so sorry if Sheeba freaked you out." Eavha set the tray on Sophie's bedside table. "Isn't freak out such a marvelous human phrase?" She let out a giggle. "My friend Tia taught me all the best human slang she learned from her mother, Queen Brea. Well, she's the former queen now. Tia is Queen of Iskalt these days."

Sophie sank onto the blush-colored settee behind her, her knees still trembling from her encounter with the fierce cat, who was apparently Eavha's idea of a pet.

"What's Iskalt?" Sophie asked.

"One of the five kingdoms. Up until recently, Lenyans believed there were only the two kingdoms of Grima and Vondur. We're in the old Vondur palace, by the way." Eavha poured two cups of tea from the steaming pot, adding copious amounts of honey to each. "That was before Tierney and Keir brought the fire plains down." She piled a plate high with pinwheel sandwiches and fruit. "But that's probably more information than you wanted to know." She sighed. "I tend to babble, so you'll have to ignore me." She set the plate and a cup of tea in front of Sophie.

"Did you say five kingdoms? That seems like a lot."

"It is. The fae world is far larger than we once thought, but the wonderful thing about our new discoveries is how united we all are now. Keir says the peace we've earned will do more healing than the healing pools themselves. And that's saying a lot because our healing pools have become quite powerful, as you can attest."

"Who is Keir?" Sophie asked, trying not to let her hunger get the better of her. She didn't know much about the fae world, but she knew a human couldn't eat their food or ... bad things would happen.

"My brother, the former King of Vondur and current husband to the Queen of Iskalt."

"Your brother is a king? Doesn't that make you a princess?"

"Vondur doesn't exist anymore. Neither goes Grima. We are all Lenyans now, and that means more to me than the title of princess ever did. Queen Bronagh has made me and my husband custodians of the region. I'm called a duchess now, I suppose." She waved a hand like that was of little consequence. "Eat, Sophie, you must be starving."

She was, but she refused to touch a morsel on her plate.

"I must get home as soon as possible. My father will be beside himself when he realizes I've been gone all night."

"All night?" Eavha stared blankly at her. "Sophie, you've been sleeping for three days. Now, you must eat and replenish yourself before you can think of leaving."

"I can't." She shoved the plate away from her just as her stomach gave an audible growl.

"Why not? Clearly, you are hungry, and you must be terribly thirsty too."

"It's not safe. For a human, I mean."

"However do you mean?" Eavha took a sip of her tea.

"All the stories say humans who eat fae food will ..." She trailed off, uncertain what the stories actually said. "It will end badly for them," she finished lamely.

"Oh, I've heard all about human fantasy stories from Gullie and Tia. They're positively hilarious." Eavha dissolved into a fit of giggles. "And purely fiction. I promise, on my honor, the food is just food. Very similar to what you might eat in your world, though I'm told Vondurian food is spicier than most other fae like. Though, Queen Alona quite enjoyed our fare when she came for a visit, and she is human."

"You have a human queen?" Sophie gasped.

Eavha nodded. "Alona is Queen of Eldur. She was a changeling child taken from the human realm—from a place called Ohio—when she was a babe and switched with a fae child to protect her. Both of them, actually. Alona's human parents were dreadful people. She grew up as a princess of Eldur and is now their beloved queen. But that is a fascinating tale for another time. Please eat, and do not worry that any harm will come to you while you're here in Lenya. As soon as we can return you to your people, you'll be on your way."

Sophie picked up her plate and sniffed the contents. It smelled delicious, and she loved spicy food.

"Watch out for the purple peppers; those are very hot. I forgot how much Gullie and Tia hate them, or I would have asked the cook to leave them off."

"It's okay. I like hot peppers." She nibbled on the edge of a sandwich and moaned. The sausage and peppers had a familiar flavor, but there was something exotic about it at the same time. She'd eaten two of the small pinwheels before she could think better of it.

"I'll ring for something cool to drink." Eavha pulled the

cord by Sophie's bed, and a moment later, a maid popped in carrying a tray.

"I thought the young miss might like some iced berry tea." She set the tray on the table between Eavha and Sophie.

"Thank you, Ariella." Eavha nodded, and the girl bobbed back out of the room.

Eavha poured the pink drink over strange-looking chunks of ice. "We've only recently been introduced to Iskalt's wonderful ice. Everyone in the palace is obsessed with cool drinks now."

Sophie took a careful sip of the drink. It was like strawberry lemonade, and it was wonderful. She chugged the whole glass and wiped her mouth. "That was delicious."

"Isn't it?" Eavha smiled as she poured Sophie another glass. "Drink as much as you like. We have plenty for everyone, and that's not something I've been able to say here for a very long time."

Eavha seemed so happy, and there was something trustworthy about her. Sophie couldn't help but wonder if all fae were like Eavha and Gulliver and maybe her father had been dead wrong about them all along.

Gulliver. She shuddered at the memory of his tail and strange cat eyes. She couldn't seem to reconcile the odd features with the nice young man she'd known in the human realm. The one she'd thought she could maybe sort of have feelings for in a world where she wasn't dying.

But was she still dying? Or was she healed by some magic she couldn't comprehend?

"Am I truly healed?" she blurted the question she'd

wanted to ask the moment she woke up feeling so much better.

"It will be difficult to know for sure, but you look like the picture of health to me." Eavha smiled and smacked her lips after a sip of the sweet drink. "Compared to the state you were in when Gullie ran through the palace screaming for help, I'd say there's a pretty good chance you're all better now. He was so distraught when he arrived, and we got you into the healing pool just in time. For a moment, we'd thought it was too late. I believe you were on death's door. At any rate, Gulliver saved your life by bringing you here. Whether that is a permanent state, I don't know."

Could it be so easy? Sophie held her breath, not wanting to believe it and then have her hopes dashed when the leukemia returned and took her life anyway. Could a person really take a bath in a fae pool and walk out completely healed from end-stage cancer?

"Gullie, don't lurk in the hallway. It's rude," Eavha called out, glancing at the shadow of two feet under the door.

He pushed the door open but still didn't enter Sophie's bedroom. His head hung low, and he refused to look at either Sophie or Eavha. His tail swished behind him like an agitated cat's.

"You're not dying anymore." He shuffled into the room.

"I'll just leave you two to catch up." Eavha slipped past Gulliver, laying a kind hand on his shoulder as she passed.

"How do you know?" Sophie asked, fussing with the linen napkin in her lap. She was suddenly nervous to be left alone with a strange man. She glanced up and met his concerned gaze. He wasn't really a stranger though, was he? She'd known him for weeks and looked forward to his visits at the cafe. But this version of him scared her. Had he only wanted to get close to her to reach her father?

"I've seen you there in New Orleans, and I've watched over you here in Lenya. You've been sleeping, but you're so much better, Sophie. I have no doubt in my mind that it will last, and you will get to live the life you should have had all along."

"I need to go home," she said firmly. "Immediately."

He nodded. "I will take you home as soon as I'm able."

"I want to go now." Her pulse pounded with fury. "Open one of your portal thingies and take me home. Now."

"I can't."

"You won't." She narrowed her eyes at him.

"No, I literally can't open a portal. Only O'Sheas have the ability to open portals—blood born O'Sheas, I mean. My father was supposed to come yesterday to check on us and take you home." Gulliver's feline eyes filled with worry. "I just left him there." His shoulders drooped.

"Is he just late?" Sophie's voice softened at the look of fear on his face.

Gulliver shook his head. "When my father makes me a promise, he keeps it. Nothing would have stopped him from coming to meet us when he said he would. Unless something terrible has happened."

She didn't think about it before she reached for his hand. Not until her skin met his and she flinched away. "What does that mean for me? Am I stuck here?" She forced a firm tone, refusing to let herself feel sorry for a man she wasn't sure she could trust.

"No. But if he doesn't show up soon, we will have to travel to Iskalt. Technically, Tia can open portals, but she's really bad at it. Her little sister is just learning how now that she's inherited her magic."

At her look of confusion, he explained, "Most fae don't get their magic until they come of age. Usually around the age of eighteen. Princess Kayleigh has had her magic for a bit now, but she's only successfully opened a portal on her own a few times. She's our best shot until the three O'Sheas currently in the human realm decide to come home."

"How long will it take to reach Iskalt?"

Gulliver sighed. "We can go by ship. It's faster, but it's still a difficult journey through the Vale of Storms. There used to be a violent maelstrom that blocked the sea path to Iskalt, but it's been healed now. We thought the vale would also calm, but it hasn't. We will have to sail around it, and that could take weeks."

"*Weeks?*" Sophie paled. "Gulliver, if my father doesn't murder you, I will."

Chapter Twenty-Five
GULLIVER

Gulliver wasn't sure what he'd hoped for. That the girl raised to hate fae would look at his extremely fae features and be so overcome with gratitude she wouldn't see him any differently? It was ridiculous.

Sophie wasn't sick anymore. Eavha didn't seem sure about that, but he knew it. In his heart, he knew Sophie had so much more to give both worlds and now she had the time to do it.

But that look in her eyes was one he'd seen too many times before. Even in most of the fae lands, they looked at Gullie with his tail and cat-like eyes and backed away. Myrkur was the only kingdom where anyone understood him. There, everyone was different.

If Sophie was truly healed, she wasn't different anymore. She could choose to be just like everyone else, to fit in and be happy. Without him.

Gulliver paced the courtyard, trying not to feel bad for himself. This palace always brought out the worst feelings in him. He couldn't stand here and not see the scaffolding that once stood at the other end of the courtyard.

Bringing a hand up, he rubbed his throat as if the fibers of the rope still scraped against his skin. His hands were smooth now, the callouses mostly healed after so long without wielding a sword, but when he looked at them, a flash of dirt-crusted, cracked palms made him stumble back.

Stone walls rose up around him, and he shook his head, trying to rid himself of the dungeon that wasn't there. But hopelessness wasn't a place. One couldn't walk away from it as easily as they could from their false imprisonment. It lived in him, spreading with every beat of his heart.

"What are you doing out here?" A familiar voice brought him back from the edge, and Gulliver turned to Declan.

"About time you showed up." Gulliver bent at the waist in a mock bow. "Your Grace." Declan hated his title, hated that it put him at a level above the common Lenyans he'd grown up beside. He wasn't born for riches and palaces, but he had been born to lead.

Declan swatted Gulliver's head and scowled. "Stop that." Through Gulliver's duties for the crowns of both Myrkur and Iskalt over the months, he'd crossed paths with Declan a few times. Despite the man's seriousness, Gulliver liked him. He'd never forget that Declan once risked his life for him or that he'd stood right beside him at the gallows.

"Anything you say, *My Lord.*"

A low growl emanated from his throat. "Don't be a fool, *Lord* Gulliver."

"But then, where would my favorite Lenyans find their entertainment?" It was so easy for Gulliver to slip back into the laughable fellow to hide what he was really thinking. Tia did the same thing, resorting to jokes, sarcasm, and humanisms to overcome dark thoughts. It drove Keir nuts when they were both together.

Declan lifted his eyes to the night sky. Thousands of stars dotted the heavens, casting Lenya in their glow. Despite the painful past here, Gulliver always loved that about Lenya. There was no other place in the fae realms with such clear nights now that the fire plains were no more. "I didn't believe Eavha when she told me you were here with a human."

"Yeah? Where have you been anyway?" Deflecting was a talent. "It's been days. I was starting to wonder if you'd fallen down that terrible staircase Keir once forced us onto and now floated down the river."

Declan finally cracked a smile. "My queen demands a lot from her vassals."

Gulliver snorted. "Bronagh would be an easy queen to serve compared to Tia. Did you know she's had me in the human realm for weeks?"

Declan winced. "My apologies. That's worse than sitting in the Vondurian dungeons."

"Thanks for the reminder that this place is terrible."

"Too soon?"

"Just a bit." Gulliver walked forward to the wall near the gate that had been closed for the night. He sat on the dusty ground and rested his back against the newly repaired stone.

Declan sighed, sitting next to him. "I've been at the

queen's palace for a council meeting. Your turn. Why would Tia send you to the humans?"

"Bronagh didn't inform you? They're killing fae." He scrubbed a hand over his face. "And I didn't manage to do a thing to stop them. I failed. Completely."

They were both quiet for a long moment before Declan spoke again. "And the girl? The one I hear you ran into the palace screaming about."

"I wasn't screaming."

"Gulliver ..."

"She ..." He sighed, wondering what she'd ever be to him. He'd never regret saving her, but he'd barely been able to visit her room because of the disgust in her eyes when she looked at him. The fear. "Her father leads the humans who are killing fae."

Declan whistled. "So, you've abducted her?"

"No!" That was exactly what he'd done.

"She chose to come with you?"

"Fine, yes. My father and I broke into a human healing ward and took her through a portal right into Lenya. She was dying, Declan. Actively dying. As in, she had minutes left. Seconds. I thought I was too late, that the healing pools wouldn't work. But they did. I would abduct her all over again if it meant she got to live."

"Sounds like you care about her."

Gulliver only glared at him.

"Are you going to use her?" he asked.

"What does that mean?"

Declan leveled him with a stare that seemed to say he shouldn't have to explain it. "Her father is killing fae and instructing others to do so. He's effectively starting a human and fae war. You have his daughter. Are you going to use her against him?"

"I ..." Was he? Could he? Sophie wanted nothing to do with Gulliver, but that didn't mean he could treat her like a bargaining chip. That wasn't why he'd fallen for her, why he'd saved her. But there were a lot of lives on the line. "I don't know."

Nodding, Declan sighed. "Eavha is pregnant."

Glad for the distraction, Gulliver perked up. "Really? That's fantastic. Congratulations."

"I grew up during a never-ending war. I don't want that for my child."

His meaning was clear. A war with humans would only hurt them, hurt future generations. "I don't know what to do."

"You'll figure it out." He patted Gulliver's leg and stood. "If Tia sent you to the human realm, she trusts you to do what's best for our world."

As soon as Declan walked away, Gulliver could no longer stand this courtyard or the stars overhead. He wasn't even sure he wanted his own company.

Jumping to his feet, he headed for the one person who hated him more than he hated himself right now. He was a sucker for pain, apparently.

When he reached Sophie's door, Eavha was coming out of it, carrying a mostly full tea tray. If Gulliver's stomach wasn't twisted in knots, he'd reach out and snag one or five of those pastries. Eating always gave him comfort, but he couldn't even allow that for himself.

"What are you doing serving her yourself?" he asked, stopping in front of the duchess.

Eavha shrugged. "I don't mind. She's still so freaked out that I thought it would be better to expose her to fewer fae. Just me and my maid are allowed in there. And you, of course, though you come mostly when she's sleeping or leave after brief conversations."

"She doesn't want me in there."

"True." Eavha didn't soften her blows. "But that's only temporary. She's mad about the delay in her return home. Let her come to terms with the trip to Iskalt and how long she will have to be in the fae realm before she's forced to deal with a man she thinks betrayed her."

"But I—"

"Saved her. Yes, I know. And she does too. Don't mistake her fear for being ungrateful." She set the tea tray on the floor by the closed door. "I am not carrying that all the way to the kitchens. Come with me. I have some Gelsi berry wine hidden away."

Gulliver fell in step beside her. "Why is it hidden?"

"My husband would drink it." She smirked.

"But you're..."

She stopped, turning to him. "He told you." She crossed her arms over her chest.

"Uh, yes?"

"That's just great. I don't even get to break the news myself. Now, he definitely doesn't get the wine. And for the record, no, I'm not going to drink it. I'm saving most of it for after this baby stops using my body like its own personal healing bath. You, on the other hand, definitely need a drink. But only one. We all know how well you hold your wine."

Gulliver couldn't argue with that. They made their way to what was once Eavha's father's rooms and then Keir's.

Now, all darkness was gone, and the once morose space was awash in color.

The mahogany bed had been replaced with one of lighter wood. Everywhere he looked there were flowers of varying colors from each of the kingdoms.

Eavha smiled when she caught him looking around. "I like to remind myself that we aren't alone in the fae world any longer." She dug through a wooden chest stuffed with clothing. "Got it." She pulled out a full bottle of brilliantly purple wine. It seemed to swirl with color in the bottle, the nature of Gelsi berries.

Most fae couldn't eat them because they dampened magical ability, but they had no effect on Dark Fae. Nor on Lenyans, who derived their power from crystals. It opened up an entirely new market for the delicacy.

Eavha retrieved a small glass goblet from a shelf, filled it with wine, and passed it to him. She brought the bottle to her nose and inhaled with her eyes shut. "One day," she whispered. "You and I will be back together again." Reluctantly, she pushed the cork back in and stashed it where presumably Declan wouldn't find it.

"Drink up." Eavha watched him intently while he sipped the wine.

"Why do I feel like you're trying to soften me?" Gulliver let the flavors burst on his tongue in a symphony he'd missed. There was nothing in any world like Gelsi berries.

"Because I am." She gestured to a cream settee before folding her skirt behind her legs and taking a seat herself.

Gulliver hesitated before joining her.

"We need to talk about Sophie's unique position as one

of very few humans who have ever gotten a glimpse of the fae realm."

He'd known this was coming since the day at the healing pools. Wandering the palace while waiting for Sophie to wake had given him a lot of time to think, and yet, he'd come to no conclusions.

"Declan wants me to use her to prevent a war."

Eavha rolled her eyes. "Such a man thing to say." She reached out and put a hand on Gulliver's arm. "Honey, we don't use innocent women for our own gain."

"I know." He rubbed his eyes. "But what about the innocent fae in the human realm being blown to bits by HAFS?" He took a long sip from his pitifully small glass of wine.

"I'm guessing this ... HAFS is the group targeting our kind?"

"Yeppers." He nodded, smacking his lips. "And Sophie's dad is their leader."

"Oh dear." Eavha sucked in a fortifying breath. "Well, if a war can be prevented by the abduction of one girl—which I'm not convinced it can be—then there has to be another way as well. Has Sophie taken part in these attacks?"

"No, no. Nope." Gulliver was quick to shake his head. "Pretty sure she hates all the violenshe," he slurred.

"I hadn't thought so." Eavha pursed her lips, urging him to slow down on the wine. "She seems ... sweet. For a human, at least."

"She is. I couldn't stay away from her. She's so pretty and kind. And she ... she looked at me like I wash normal." He hung his head, letting the last of the wine swirl in his glass. "Tia shent me to New Orleans for a job, and I didn't do it because of Sho-phie. Wh-what if I'm the reashon some of those fae are dead?"

Eavha squeezed his free hand and plucked the nearly empty glass from his other. "You really can't hold your wine, can you?" She gave him a sad smile. "I have a better question for you. What if you're the reason even more fae in the human realm *won't* die? Gullie, all we can control is our future because the past has already been written. So, what really matters is what you do next."

Gulliver tilted his head, studying the former Princess of Vondur. "When did you grow up?" Eavha had always been kind, but she spoke with a calmness and maturity she hadn't had before.

"I'm a duchess now." She laughed. "That comes with real responsibility." Growing up as a princess meant little in Vondur. She hadn't been afforded any responsibilities or duties just because her father was the king. Now, she had a purpose.

"I need to let Sophie choose her own path." His shoulders drooped. He'd suffered as a prisoner and could never imagine holding anyone against their will. "If she wishes to return home, we'll travel to Iskalt so an O'Shea can open a portal for us." Right now, those he trusted to reliably open portals were in the human realm, but there were others.

"You'll have a bigger obstacle once you get there."

"Tia." He took the glass back from Eavha and drained the rest of his wine. The liquid buzzed through him, but it didn't give him the warmth he expected. He bent forward, putting his head in his hands. "This is the first time I can't anticipate what she's going to do."

Scold him? Demand access to Sophie to save the fae in

the human realm? Would she even allow Sophie to return home after witnessing the kind of healing magic humans might kill for?

"Tia will do what is best." Eavha had so much faith in her. Gulliver did too, but he also knew her.

"No. Tierney O'Shea will always do what she *thinks* is best." Those weren't always the same thing.

Chapter Twenty-Six
SOPHIE-ANN

This place was straight out of a story—the kind her father never let her read growing up. It didn't mean she hadn't. Reading fantasy novels had been Sophie's one rebellion. In their house, magic was evil, something to eradicate from the world.

Until she was older, Sophie hadn't known just how real that magic was. Her father kept the truth from her until she was ready, making up stories about what created the dark months, but how does one ever prepare for that kind of revelation? That her father wasn't just an eccentric old man, but rather the leader of a radical and violent organization who knew things about the world most turned a blind eye to?

"Where am I?" Sophie whispered to herself as she stopped, realizing just how lost she was.

Needing to clear her head, she'd tried the door to her room and was surprised to find it unlocked. So much for keeping an eye on their prisoner. There were fewer servants than she'd expected and none in this part of the castle.

The royal residence behind her, she kept walking until she didn't know how many turns she'd taken. This place was huge, but it had obviously been a long time since anyone used this wing.

Broken stone coated the floor like a layer of lost dreams. She ran her hand along the black scorch marks reaching toward a ceiling held up by only the occasional wooden beam. How did the roof remain overhead with so little support?

Something happened here. Something bad. She looked back over her shoulder to make sure no one followed her before turning into the largest room she'd seen yet. Shreds of carpeting stood out as the only color in the otherwise grim room. Sunlight streamed in through arched windows, casting the shadows aside to reveal a tarnished seat.

"A throne." Her eyes widened as she neared it. This was a throne room. Bending, she picked up a scrap of carpet that was singed at the edges and ran her fingers over it. Velvet. Closing her eyes, she pictured what this place once was, a bustling center of activity for a powerful kingdom. She saw kings and queens alike taking that throne as their own, fighting for their might.

From the looks of things, the story of Lenya wasn't a fairytale. It was a tragedy.

Taking the steps up to the throne slowly, she lowered herself onto it, wondering what it was like to have any power at all. She'd spent her life at the mercy of her illness, of her father's whims. Even at her death, he demanded she marry to cement his legacy.

She brushed rubble from the arms of the throne and leaned back, seeing the room from a new view, with velvet carpeting stretching from the door and brightly dressed courtiers elbowing each other for their sovereign's attention.

Yes, your Majesty. No, your Majesty.

Yes, Father. No, Father.

It was all the same. She'd wanted him to love her, to trust her. So, she kept her mouth shut as HAFS destroyed lives, created havoc. Even if she could tell herself they only ever hurt fae, how could she justify that now? If their kindness was any indication, they weren't the barbarous race she'd believed.

Yet, they also weren't human. Magic wasn't natural. No man should have a tail sprouting from his butt.

"Mom," she said, "I don't know if you can hear me in this world, but I don't know what to do, how to get home." She waited for the comfort of knowing her mother was there with her, but all she felt was a seeping cold. Her mother wouldn't follow her into a world full of the creatures that caused her death.

And Sophie shouldn't be here either.

"They saved my life, Mom." How could that kind of magic be sinful? She should be long dead now, free from the human world and sitting at her mother's side. But as much as she wished for that reunion, she wasn't ready. "I'm still alive." A tear tracked down her cheek, and she let it fall. She was alive and healthy for the first time in as long as she could remember.

Was it a miracle or a curse? Those she needed to hate were the very ones who gave her life back to her.

Yet, it wasn't only that. Here, so far from New Orleans,

she could feel pieces of her heart stitch themselves back together. Every time her father and the group she too belonged to hurt others, it tore at her. She could still see the faces of those suspected of being fae, the ones HAFS made examples of. Could still hear the gunshots, the thud of their bodies hitting the ground.

But here, their lives didn't weigh on her. She had space to think, to search for some kind of clarity in the mess both worlds had become. The sins of her father were not her own; those faults did not belong on her shoulders.

Staying silent did.

She vowed to change if they ever allowed her to go home. No more indiscriminate killing, random bombing. Those were the acts of terrorists, and she refused to let her father's anger and grief take him further down that path than he could return from.

"I always wondered what it would be like to belong in that chair," Eavha spoke from the doorway, arms crossed over her chest.

Sophie sat up quickly. "I'm sorry, I—"

Eavha waved away her apology. "By all means, stay there for a moment. It was never my throne. Here in Vondur—what this kingdom was called before simply becoming part of Lenya—the crown was taken by force. Death. As much as I'd have liked to see the world from the height of power, I never would have been willing to do what was needed to get there."

Nausea curled in Sophie's stomach. Like so many other things, it was a throne stained in blood. "What happened in this place?" She gestured around to what once must have been a grand room.

Eavha sighed and stepped closer. "A battle. One in which we were victorious."

This was what victory looked like? "Who did you fight?"

"Not who. What. A great wave of heat threatened to turn all of Lenya into a wasteland of ash and bone." One corner of her mouth curved up. "But the five kingdoms worked together and managed to win the day with our magic. We've only managed to restore a small part of this castle, but we will keep going. It's honestly amazing this room still has a roof. Most in this part of the castle is open to the elements."

Sophie couldn't help wanting to know more, to understand this world and what it had been through. Yet, the questions couldn't break through her determination to hate it. "Are we in danger here?"

"Probably." Eavha shrugged. "The roof is still there, mostly, but the wooden beams are now ash underneath our feet."

"Yet, you still came here."

"Sophie-Ann ... Gullie told me that's your full name. Is it okay if I use it?"

Sophie nodded, shrinking back at the mention of Gulliver.

"It's a beautiful name. Anyway, Sophie-Ann, I live in a palace that is half in ruin with only a few maids, a household guard, and a host of refugees when my husband is away. We are not even a year displaced from a civil war that lasted far longer than you can fathom. We've faced famine, the fire plains, and learning of four kingdoms we didn't think existed."

"I don't understand most of what you just said."

Eavha smirked. "What I'm getting at is, Lenyans aren't scared of anything, not anymore. We've already faced the worst. So, if I wish to walk around the old part of the castle and remember what it once was, I will."

What was it like not to fear? For so long, Sophie went to bed each night wondering if she'd wake up in the morning. She worked at the cafe when she shouldn't have because being alone while her father worked was terrifying. She'd never been as scared of anything as she was of herself. "That sounds wonderful. Not living in fear."

Eavha sighed and lowered herself to sit on the step in front of the throne, right in the dust. "You do not have to fear us."

"I don't."

"And you also do not have to lie." She shook her head. "Gulliver would not have brought you here if he did not think you'd be able to understand what it is we are."

"And what is that?"

"Not human, that's for sure. But there's a reason we can pass so easily. We are a sophisticated species. We love and hate and are quick to both anger and forgiveness. Fae make mistakes, just as humans do. We are not so different."

"But Gulliver ..."

"Is not so different." This time when Eavha said it, there was more emphasis on the words, almost an anger behind them.

Sophie leaned her head back. "He tricked me. That's what fae do, isn't it? He chose me because of who my father is."

"And he failed his queen because he chose to save your life over the mission she sent him on."

They locked eyes, and Sophie couldn't look away. "A queen sent him ..."

"Not just any queen. Tierney of Iskalt. She is the most powerful magic wielder in the five kingdoms and also the most important fae in Gulliver's life. Those two ... Let's just say Tia has no more loyal friend."

Gulliver was an arm of a queen. Sophie wasn't sure if she should feel comforted or angry. He deceived her, played her because the fae were operating missions in the human realm. They didn't belong there, just as she didn't belong here in their world.

If Eavha thought she could tell tales of the great Gulliver and make her see him as something other than the beast who betrayed her, she was wrong. He was nothing more than a fae spy.

She left the woman to her thoughts in that dangerous throne room and managed to make her way back to the residence wing with the help of a maid Gulliver sent to look for her.

He was waiting outside her door when she arrived. "Not now, Gullie." She tried to push past him, but he stopped her with a hand on her arm.

"Where were you?"

Yanking herself free, she shoved open the door. "Trying to make myself forget just where I am." With that, she shut the door in his face, hiding her tears from him.

She kicked off her boots and pulled at the laces of the silly dress they'd given her to wear. They'd even made her wear a corset—the most vile, uncomfortable creation any world had ever known. Finally getting the contraption loose, she slid the corset and dress down her legs and drew in a deep breath, her chest heaving for more oxygen.

Breathe. She had to breathe.

She grasped the bedpost to stabilize herself and clutched her waist with the other hand. The silken underthings she wore were cool against her heated skin, but it wasn't enough.

Rushing to the bathroom, she searched for anything to calm her down, to make her forget. But all she found was a basin of water left over from her morning bath.

Without thinking, she dropped to her knees and plunged her head in, letting cold water trickle down her back. Silk clung to her skin as she flipped her hair back, and her breathing returned to normal. *You're an idiot, Sophie.*

Before she had a chance to dry herself, her door burst open. "You have to talk to me." Gulliver froze, his eyes trailing the length of her in open shock and dismay. A tiny squeak escaped his lips, and she worried he was going to pass out right there on the spot.

Chapter Twenty-Seven
GULLIVER

"Your skin looks so soft." Gullie slapped a hand over his mouth to keep himself from blurting out anything even more embarrassing. He whirled around to face the door, stammering something unintelligible. "I'm sorry, Sophie! I didn't mean to barge in. Didn't mean to stare." He covered his eyes but couldn't seem to make his feet move to leave the poor girl alone.

"What are you babbling about?" Sophie sounded irritated.

"Are you decent? I need to talk to you about the journey to Iskalt."

She heaved a sigh he heard in his bones. Fae she was mad at him. "Of course I'm decent."

Gulliver slowly turned around to find her still sopping wet standing with her hands on her hips and glaring daggers at him.

"I told you I wasn't in the mood to talk to you, so make it

quick. When are we leaving? And why are you facing the door again?"

Sometime in her yelling at him, he'd turned his back to her once more. "I thought you said you were decent." Heat crept up his neck, and he could feel his ears turning scarlet.

"I am. I just had a little dunk in the wash basin to cool off. I'm better now."

"But you're in your underthings, Soph." His voice squeaked, and he rolled his eyes at himself, his tail twitching in agitation.

"I have more clothes on now than at any time you saw me in New Orleans. I wear shorts and t-shirts."

"But you're ... you're all ... wet, and things are ... sticking." He covered his flaming face with his hands. *You're such an idiot, Gulliver.*

She gasped, but Gullie still didn't turn around. "Can you see through everything?" He heard rustling sounds as she crossed the room to the mirror in the corner by the dressing screen. "Gulliver," she groaned, "you can't see anything but my belly button, you dork. You'd see more of me in a bathing suit. Now, turn around and say whatever you came to say."

"It's fine; I can just talk to the door." He crossed his arms over his chest, refusing to look at any woman in such a state of undress. It wasn't gentlemanly behavior.

"Now, wait just a minute. I am not indecent! I'm covered from neck to toes in this awful underdress thing."

"It's a shift, and it's wet, and I can see your under-under things." For the first time in his life, he really wished he had magic so he could vanish in a poof of blazing light. Not that he'd ever seen a single fae do such a thing. Tia probably could manage it if she wanted to, but she didn't really get embarrassed.

"Okay. Whatever this sack dress is, it's not much different than the one I had on when I came into my room. Are you seriously not going to turn around and look at me?"

"Nope." He shook his head. "Could you just put on a robe or something? I'm trying to be a gentleman here."

"Oh for heaven's sake. What you're being is ridiculous."

Gullie couldn't tell what she was doing, but he wasn't about to turn around until he was certain his eyes would stay in his head and focused on her face and not on other parts of her.

"There is nothing immodest about a woman's body in a shift. Even if it is a little damp."

"You aren't wearing a ... a *corset*." He whispered the last word like he was ten and didn't know anything about women. Well, he was twenty-two and didn't know anything about women, but that was beside the point.

"No, and I don't plan on wearing one ever again, so get used to it. That thing was suffocating the life out of me."

He heard more rustling and the sound of fabric hitting the floor.

"You'd think fae women would just magic them in place rather than wear a torture device probably invented by a man." Her voice was muffled, and he prayed she was putting on several more layers.

Gullie flinched when she threw something wet at him and it landed on his head. He pulled the fabric away and leaped toward the door when he realized he was holding the only stitch of actual clothing she'd had on.

Her laughter followed him, and he stopped with his

hand on the doorknob, his shoulders falling and his face flaming. "You're just making fun of me now, aren't you?"

"You do make it easy. You can turn around now. I'm in my robe, still fully covered from neck to toes in a non-see-through shade of purple."

"Are you sure?"

"Positive. Now, tell me whatever you came to tell me and leave. I have to pack for this *weeks*-long trip you subjected me to when you brought me here against my will."

"But I—"

She held up a hand to stop him. "Saved my life? Yes, I know, and don't think I'm not grateful for it. I just really don't like it when men and … *fae* make decisions for me without asking what I want. I'm tired of it."

"I understand." Gulliver dropped his head, not sure how he would ever make this right or if she would always see him as a monster who took away her free will. "I'll just go." His tail dragged behind him as he opened the door.

"Wait," Sophie called after him.

He turned around, hope in his eyes. "Yes?"

"You came here to tell me something about our trip to Iskalt. Have you figured out how to fly us there or something hopefully as fast?"

"I-I don't have wings. Though, my mother and sisters do. But they're in Myrkur."

"So …?" She seemed to be growing more irritable with him as the seconds wore on.

"Um, just, we will be leaving by ship in four days."

"I can't wait that long. I have to get home before my father does something drastic."

Gullie gulped a breath before he continued in a rush,

"Well, you see … um, the shores of Vondur are too shallow for most ships. Um, so we have to travel east to the palace of Lenya. It takes three days to reach the new palace over land."

"I assume we're going by some sort of fae version of a car, right?"

Gulliver shook his head. "Um … not exactly. We … um … we tend not to move as fast as humans do. We live more simply. Unless it's an emergency, and then we use portals."

"And that means what?" She prodded him, forcing a patient tone he knew she didn't feel.

"Horses," he blurted. "We will travel on horseback. Er, just the two of us. I've, uh, made the trip many times, so we won't get lost or anything."

"Gullie! I've never ridden a horse in my life."

"Really?" His eyes widened at the look of menace on her face. "We can take a wagon if you'd be more comfortable, but it will be slower. Or if you're worried about traveling with me alone, I can ask Declan to escort us. You can ride with him if you feel safer that way."

"It's fine. I'll manage."

Gulliver took a hasty step toward the door, hoping for a quick escape before he had to tell her how much harder this trip would get when they had to go around the far northern reaches of Iskalt they'd discovered after the fall of the Vatlands. It was an insanely cold and treacherous path. "We'll leave tomorrow. So, um, just let me know if you need anything. Eavha is packing some travel clothes for you."

"Honestly, for a fae with magic, you're kind of hopeless."

"I-I'm sorry. I thought you knew. I don't actually have magic." He halted in the doorway of her room. "Dark Fae have defensive magic only. Meaning magic doesn't really work on us. It's kind of like armor, so magic just kind of bounces off me. It's also what makes me look ... normal in the human world. Other than that, I have no more magic than you do, Sophie."

"Oh. I see." Her face paled, and the tension seemed to leave her body.

Gulliver fled the room as quickly as his feet could carry him. He couldn't stand the strange look on her face a moment longer.

Feeling defeated and uncertain of what to expect when he arrived unannounced at the palace in Iskalt with a human woman in tow, Gulliver sought the privacy of his room. He was itching to leave Vondur as soon as possible. The palace brought nothing but bad memories, and he was eager to make things right for Sophie.

Reaching for his pack under the bed, he started tossing things haphazardly into his bag. He wouldn't need much on the journey. Just plenty of food and water. This side of Lenya was still hot. Nothing like it had been when the fire plains caused temperatures to rise, but the southwestern lands were similar to Eldur in temperature and in landscape, if a bit milder in comparison.

Judging by their conversation this afternoon, it was going to be a long journey with just the two of them. And there would be hell to pay when Tia found out what he'd done.

His hand landed on something he'd forgotten about at the bottom of his pack. The spelled journal his father had given him so he could communicate with Tia.

That was days and days ago. He sucked in a breath and sat on the bed, fully prepared for an earful when he opened the book and found a page of messages from Tia.

. . .

Gullie, how are things going in the human world? I'm anxiously awaiting news.

Gullie? Is everything okay?

Gulliver Muriel O'Shea, where are you? Your queen demands an update.

Gulliver snorted at that. He didn't have a middle name. That was more of a human thing Brea had brought into fashion when she named her children. It was all the rage now across the kingdoms. When they were kids, Tia had felt bad he didn't have one, so she gave him one. Back then, it was Alexander, which he quite liked, and if anyone asked him if he had a middle name, that's the one he gave. But whenever Tia was really mad at him, she three named him with whatever insulting name she could come up with in that moment.

Muriel? Really, Tia? I've been a bit busy, and though you are my best friend and a queen I admire, you are technically not my queen, as I am from Myrkur. He slammed the book closed and went back to packing his few belongings. He loved Tia, but sometimes she was infuriating with her demands.

The journal started to smoke and spark on his bed, and he leaped for it, stamping out the smoldering blanket. "For the love of magic, Tia, learn some patience!" He flipped to the last page he wrote on and waited for the words to scrawl across the page.

What is going on? Why haven't you responded, Gul. It's been too long since Griffin left. I demand an update.

Gulliver's blood boiled as he snatched up a quill and began to write.

Tierney James O'Shea, sometimes a fae can't be at your

beck and call every moment of the day. I forgot about the book till just now. It's been difficult the past few days.

James? That's the best you could come up with?

Gulliver dreaded the next part. Telling her everything he'd done and how he needed her to help fix his mess.

Tia, don't get mad. I'm in our least favorite place in all the worlds, and I desperately need you ...

Chapter Twenty-Eight
TOBY

"Toby, get down!" Xavier nearly tackled him in the darkness, pulling him out of the human's way. They were everywhere.

"What do we do?" Toby panted, his eyes searching the dark for the source of all the noise and sparks of human magic he didn't understand. Fae were running from their homes in the middle of the night, trying to flee the attack.

"I don't know how they found us," Xavier whispered in his ear as they cowered behind the well house in the town square. "This village is protected. Only one of our own could have led them here."

"We have to fight back." Toby wrestled away from his embrace. "We can't let them win."

"We don't have weapons." Xavier lunged after him, but Toby had already found his target. A human boy not much younger than himself backed toward them, his odd human sword pointed in the wrong direction.

Toby charged him, landing a forceful blow against his shoulder.

"They have guns!" Xavier shrieked, though Toby didn't know what a gun was.

"There are children here!" Toby pushed his opponent to the ground with a kick to his ribs. "You can't do this."

The boy turned hate-filled eyes on him. "Die, you fae freak!" He pointed his gun-sword at Toby. "If you won't go back to your own world, I'll send you there myself."

His weapon jerked, and a blast of power erupted inside Toby. He slid to the ground in a daze.

"Toby!" Xavier screamed for him, but his vision flickered and heat shot up his arm and into his chest. He couldn't breathe, and the night went silent around him.

Toby saw a figure crash into the human with the gun that wasn't just a sword, but he saw another blurry figure standing over him. One he'd know anywhere.

He reached a hand toward the man. "Logan?"

About Melissa

Melissa A. Craven is an Amazon bestselling author of Young Adult Contemporary Fiction and YA Fantasy (her Contemporary fans will know her as Ann Maree Craven). Her books focus on strong female protagonists who aren't always perfect, but they find their inner strength along the way. Melissa's novels appeal to audiences of all ages and fans of almost any genre. She believes in stories that make you think and she loves playing with foreshadowing, leaving clues and hints for the careful reader.

Melissa draws inspiration from her background in architecture and interior design to help her with the small details in world building and scene settings. Her favorite pastime is sitting on her porch when the weather is nice with her two dogs, Fynlee and Nahla, reading from her massive TBR pile and dreaming up new stories.

Visit Melissa at Melissaacraven.com for more information about her newest series and discover exclusive content.

Join our Facebook Group:
Melissa and Michelle's Fantasy Book Warriors
Follow Michelle and Melissa on TikTok at
@ATaleOfTwoAuthors

About Michelle

Michelle MacQueen is a USA Today bestselling author of love. Yes, love. Whether it be YA romance, NA romance, or fantasy romance (Under M. Lynn), she loves to make readers swoon.

The great loves of her life to this point are two tiny blond creatures who call her "aunt" and proclaim her books to be "boring books" for their lack of pictures. Yet, somehow, she still manages to love them more than chocolate.

When she's not sharing her inexhaustible wisdom with her niece and nephew, Michelle is usually lounging in her ridiculously large bean bag chair creating worlds and characters that remind her to smile every day - even when a feisty five-year-old is telling her just how much she doesn't know.

See more from M. Lynn and sign up
to receive updates and deals!
michellelynnauthor.com

Join Melissa and Michelle's Facebook Group:
Melissa and Michelle's Fantasy Book Warriors

Follow Michelle and Melissa on TikTok at
@ATaleOfTwoAuthors

More From Brea's World

Don't miss the FREE prequel,

Fae's Dilemma

Grab your copy here!

https://michellelynnauthor.com/dilemma

www.ingramcontent.com/pod-product-compliance
Lightning Source LLC
Chambersburg PA
CBHW030529310726
48979CB00010B/1853/J
* 9 7 8 1 9 7 0 0 5 2 8 9 3 *